Go for the
Honey
Winning Cathy

Charlotte S. Snead

Jan-Carol
Publishing, Inc

"every story needs a book"

Go for the Honey: Winning Cathy
Hope House Girls Series
Book 3
Charlotte S. Snead

Published June 2018
Little Creek Books
Imprint of Jan-Carol Publishing, Inc.
All rights reserved
Copyright © 2018 Charlotte S. Snead

ISBN: 978-1-945619-63-2
Library of Congress Control Number: 2018947776

You may contact the publisher:
Jan-Carol Publishing, Inc.
PO Box 701
Johnson City, TN 37605
publisher@jancarolpublishing.com
jancarolpublishing.com

*To the social workers, therapists, and housemothers
and volunteers who influence the lives of troubled girls
and lead them to victory and new life.
I have worked with women and girls facing unplanned
pregnancies since 1985. Not one of them is irredeemable.
God has a plan and a purpose for each one,
and I have seen them not only survive,
but truly thrive as God leads them into new life.*

Dear Reader

We hear a lot about sex trafficking these days. The highway rest stops even post alerts, but we know little about personal circumstances.

Cathy is such a one. A run away at fifteen, she was lured and then trapped into prostitution. As David told his father, 'She was fifteen, who would do such a thing?' Let us pray our attorney general will continue to succeed in capturing the vermin who lure girls (and boys) into their sleazy rackets.

And let us rejoice that God can make all things new. As you read *Go for the Honey*, know that nothing is impossible with God! He gave her love for the son of rape, joy in her marriage and family, enabled her, as a social worker, to rescue another young girl, and gave her the Righteousness of her Lord, a grace gift no one can earn.

"*Thy lips, O my spouse, drop as the honeycomb:*
honey and milk are under thy tongue; and the smell of thy garments
is like the smell of Lebanon.'"

—Song of Solomon 4:11 (KJV)

Brave Face

Betsy, the dorm advisor, watched as Cathy, smiling and waving, sent the last group of vacationers off. Cathy assured them her folks had just been delayed; they'd be here soon. But Betsy figured they wouldn't. Cathy had been left countless times; as usual, she was the last thing on their minds. At eight o'clock, the hall advisor approached her student, who was by this time a miserable lump on her dorm room's comfortable chair.

Noticing her tear-streaked face, the advisor squatted beside her. "Any word, Cath?"

"Nope. They aren't coming, Betts."

"Shall we contact the police?"

"No. Remember last break, when they said they'd be here and never came? They must have decided to stay longer in Aruba or Maui, wherever they are."

Betsy had seen the teenager disappointed time after time by her negligent parents in the three years she'd worked for the school, but this time it was critical. The dorm was scheduled for major work during the three-week break before fall semester, so all residents had to be out of the building. With a soft touch, Betsy reached out and swiped a tear from Cathy's left cheek.

Cathy's mouth quivered, but she bit her bottom lip and stood. "What am I going to do? I was supposed to be out of here by six, and it's eight o'clock."

Patting her knee, Betsy looked at the teen's attempt to put on a brave face while arranging her own to be cheerful. "Nothing to do except take you home with me. Come on, get your stuff." She picked up one of Cathy's suitcases, leaving the smaller one for the young teen.

"How far away do you live? Do you even have room? Don't you live with your parents? They don't know I'm coming. They won't want uninvited guests."

"Sweetie, my parents always welcome my guests. You're welcome, but it's dark, so we need to get a move on. I live in Connecticut, about three hours away. You'll be great company on the road!" Cathy sniffed, and tears continued to roll down her cheeks. "We'll have fun. Wipe those tears, now. My brothers are coming home, too. Mom will have scrumptious stuff made: cookies and pies to die for." Cathy stood, and Betsy bumped her with her hip. "Get cracking. Need to pee before we get on the road?"

The girls' tennis shoes squeaked on the spotless hall floors. They dodged around tarps and ladders set up for the renovations. A worker in coveralls asked why they were here. The building was supposed to be empty by six o'clock. Betsy apologized and put her arm around Cathy's waist, guiding her out the back door and down the steps to the parking lot.

"It's creepy in there when everyone is gone. I hate staying for holidays." Cathy shuddered.

Betsy knew she usually stayed for every one, except when she went to summer camp during the long break. "This will be fun. We're going to have a fabulous time."

And it was; Betsy's mother welcomed Cathy with a warm embrace, piling blankets and a pillow on the floor for the first night. The next day they bought out a day bed for her. Both Betsy and her mother seemed to enjoy feeding her every time she turned around so she could "fill out," because she was too thin. Betsy had fretted over this student on her dorm floor and wanted to bring her home, but Cathy's parents always refused, choosing instead to leave her in the empty dorm. She knew Cathy made up stories about her so-called vacations to tell the others, spending her holidays online researching resorts to create her fantasies.

Betsy knew her young friend was an only child in a cold, sterile mansion, and watched her marvel at the laughter in this home. Betsy, the youngest of three, was constantly teased by her two older brothers, but it was all in fun.

She'd worked hard to earn a place at the boarding school, attending the college program at the elite school.

"Listen, guys," Betsy instructed her brothers. "Cathy is an only child. She's not used to your wild ways, so cut out your teasing, you hear?" They did alter their behavior, but the fragile girl was resilient. Cathy began to banter with them by the second week, so they included her in their light-hearted fun.

For the first time in her life, Cathy attended church—a function the entire family took seriously—and she was moved by their devotion. The three weeks flew by, and when time came to return to school, Cathy cried again. After a fierce hug for Betsy's mother, she was quiet on the ride back.

Betsy pulled into the parking lot and they walked into the brightly painted dormitory together. Betsy dreaded her face-to-face with the dean. She knew she didn't have permission to take her charge home, but she insisted she'd never regret it. Betsy told Cathy, "I'm glad you came home with me. The visit was good for you. I've never seen you have so much fun. I'd never even seen you laugh!" But both girls knew what was to come; Betsy faced disciplinary action. Cathy's parents threatened a lawsuit and pulled their daughter out of the school. Betsy ended up losing her job and transferring to a community college near her home. The girls promised to keep in touch, and Cathy went home.

Father's Useful Daughter

Cathy's parents searched for other boarding schools that would take a new student at this late date, while keeping her at home and barely tolerating her presence. They left her with staff in their mansion while they attended their myriad affairs. One morning, Cathy ran into her father at breakfast. He lowered his newspaper and regarded her with surprise.

"You've grown up, Catherine. You are quite lovely—like your mother." He bellowed for his wife and she came scurrying, apologizing for being late. He waved her off. "I was early this morning. Look at her," he commanded. Placing his fingers under Cathy's chin, her father turned her head back and forth. Cathy wondered if he'd draw her lips back and examine her teeth, like he did his horses. "She's exquisite; just like you, my dear. Fix her up today. Get her to a salon and buy her a dress. I believe she'll be useful tonight." Snapping his paper, he dismissed himself from the conversation but after he rose, he stood behind Cathy's chair.

"We might send you to school nearby if you prove yourself tonight. I need you to entertain one of my investors. Ply him with compliments, hang on his arm, stare adoringly. You teach her, Audrey. You always do an excellent job."

Cathy's eyes snapped. "Do I go to bed with him, Father?"

Her father glowered, and then broke into a smile. "You are old enough to decide that for yourself. We can arrange emergency contraception, and if this works out, we'll get you on birth control."

"*Evan!*" Audrey exclaimed.

4

He regarded her with cold eyes. "Yes, my dear?"

She looked down. Cathy was hustled off to a salon, where her burnished blonde hair was highlighted and styled, her curls piled on her head. She looked at least five years older than her fifteen years, especially when fitted with padded undergarments to enhance her girlish figure and an exquisite gown. Throughout the day, her mother coached her in the fine art of conversation, telling her to focus on her father's genius, investment skills, and business acumen. Cathy always wondered why her father had married her mother. She knew her mom wasn't well educated and didn't come from her father's social class. Now, she got it. Her beautiful mother was "useful." Cathy wondered if she'd prostituted herself to his clients. During her short stays at home she'd realized her parents had separate bedrooms, but occasionally her father frequented her mother's room, often tipsy and demanding. She hated those nights.

The evening was an ordeal. Her father's client was already somewhat drunk when he arrived and became increasingly so, fawning all over Cathy. His suggestive touches made her feel nauseous. Once her father seized her arms in a bruising grip and whispered harshly, "You'd better make this look good. Smile, laugh, play with the man. Do it. Put your hand on his thigh. Now. Do you hear me? Lean toward him like you're interested. Didn't your mother teach you anything?"

The client approached the table, setting a cocktail in front of Cathy and chugging his Scotch on the rocks.

Cathy looked at her mother across the room. She was leaning toward an older man, revealing her cleavage and laughing brightly. *Gross,* Cathy thought. Obediently, under her father's careful eye, she put her hand on the older man's thigh—but as soon as her father left the table, she moved it to his arm. With a leer, he informed her he liked it better where it was and moved it back. Cathy began to have a horrible feeling about how this night would end, but she remembered Betsy's brothers joking around about a friend who was too drunk to accomplish anything when he got his girlfriend upstairs. Cathy fetched him drink after drink until she feared he'd get alcohol poisoning, but it worked; eventually, he passed out cold on the table.

Both her parents complimented her maneuvers in the limo on the way home, and they discussed the next upcoming gala as more of the same.

Cathy wouldn't be there. One night, when she knew they'd be away for hours, Cathy took the cash they'd left for staff to run the household. She'd planned her escape, watching and waiting for the opportunity. She took a small suitcase, packed with the jeans her mother hated and sweatshirts from her former school; she told the taxi driver to take her to the bus station, where she boarded the first outgoing bus, which was going to Pittsburgh. She picked up a postcard and jotted a brief note to Betsy, telling her she was fine and not to worry. Then Cathy checked into a bargain motel to ponder her next move. She ate cheap and kept most of the cash in reserve. But early the next week, she saw her face on fliers declaring her a missing minor. *Time to move on. Back to the bus station*, Cathy thought. The next departure was for Wheeling, West Virginia. She pulled her ball cap low and boarded quietly. This time, she wouldn't risk any communication with anyone, no matter how beloved—not that she loved many people.

On the Run

O nce again, she stayed at a cheap motel and hoarded her rapidly dwin-
dling stash of money. However, after a couple of weeks, she had to
check out. She wanted to find a job but if she gave out her Social Security
number, she'd be picked up—and jobs that paid under the table were hard to
come by. She joined some homeless people under a bridge, but the September wind at night in West Virginia was cold. She pulled on two sweatshirts
and added a layer of sweatpants over her jeans. She ate in a diner, only
buying enough to keep alive. Her third night there, she saw the guy behind
the corner nod his head toward her. Busted! She looked for a place to run,
but saw no cops. Instead, a middle-aged woman scooted into the booth.

"Sandy says you're looking for a job. I may be able to help."

Looking at her with skepticism, Cathy said. "No Social Security number."

"We can deal with that," she said; leaning forward, she whisper, "We
hire illegals."

"I'm not illegal. I just don't want to be found."

The woman patted her hand. "I understand. I'm Rita, and I'm the housemother for the girls who work for us. You look thin—been on the run long?"

"A month, but I'm running out of money."

"I'm sure we can find you some employment, dear, but first we need to
fatten you up. Will you come with me? I must ask Donnie. He does all the
hiring."

Cathy hesitated. "It wouldn't hurt to try, I guess."

"I'll pick up your tab. Have you finished?"

Cathy balled up her napkin and threw it on her plate. "Yes, Ma'am."

The woman's scrutiny reminded Cathy of her father, and she shivered as she walked into the rainy night.

"You don't have a coat?"

"No, Ma'am. I gave it to a homeless lady with two kids."

"We can find something to fit you at the home." She led Cathy to a luxury car.

"Nice," Cathy observed.

"You'll like the home. It's an old historic brownstone. We have about fifteen girls living there. The boys have a separate wing."

"What kind of jobs do you have?"

"Donnie will talk to you and see what you like to do. He does all the placements. We need to get some meat on your bones first! You look ill. You don't have anything contagious, do you?"

"No, Ma'am. I've been out of work and on the streets a while."

"No matter, we'll have you checked out."

Rita made many twists and turns driving to the home. Cathy was hopelessly lost, but they soon stopped in front of a beautiful house. Rita unlocked the car and urged Cathy to follow her up the broad stone stairs.

Cathy stepped into a foyer almost as magnificent as her father's mansion and looked around. She wasn't cowed by her surroundings like Rita's usual finds. "Follow me. I'll take you to your room. Do you need me to wash your clothes?"

"I can do it."

"If you like; you look tired, so I thought I'd offer. First, we'll stop at the clothing room and see if we can find something for you." Rita fitted her with a warm jacket and asked if she needed pajamas. Blinking back tears, Cathy nodded. She hadn't worn pajamas in two months. The older woman put her in a single room. "The door locks, if you'd feel more comfortable. I'll introduce you to the other girls at breakfast. Most of them are out on the town. The bathroom is down the hall." She pointed. "I'll get you your own towels—hang them on the towel rack behind your door. You look like you need a good night's sleep."

"Thank you, Rita."

"No problem. You take a hot bath and crawl in bed. No one will bother you 'til morning. I'll come get you for breakfast. Sleep tight."

Cathy stood at the door as Rita walked away, reaching for her ringing phone. "Yes, Donnie, looks like Sandy found us an excellent candidate. You'll like her. She's on the run, but classy, well-spoken, and when we fatten her up, she'll be a beauty. She's been on the streets about a couple of months. Let's wait a week or so, settle her in. She's tired and hungry. Definitely for our high-end clients." She turned the corner, and Cathy lost the rest of her conversation.

The next morning Cathy was awake before the knock on the door. She heard a commotion in the middle of the night, giggling and shushing, but she put her pillow over her head and went back to sleep. She'd been afraid in those sleazy motels, and she hadn't slept in a nice bed in a long time.

"Good morning, Cathy." Rita took her arm as she came out of the bathroom. "Hungry?"

"Yes, Ma'am. I could eat a horse."

"We have eggs and bacon. No horse, I'm afraid."

Cathy giggled. "Okay."

Rita introduced her around the table—Betty, Lorraine, Nancy—but Cathy stopped at Cindy Lou. She looked hungover, drunk, or something. She had a sloppy grin on her face and glassy eyes. Cathy was worried about her and asked Rita if she was ill. The other girls laughed.

"Girls, being sick isn't funny!" She helped Cindy Lou stand. "Come, it's back to bed for you." Rita placed a hand on her brow, ostensibly checking for fever, but the other girls exchanged knowing glances. One girl—Cathy thought her name was Doris—started to say something, but Rita glowered at her, and she turned to her breakfast.

For a week, no one mentioned work. Rita was with her throughout the day, feeding her five times every day. She allowed her to do laundry and a few chores around the place, but informed her she had to look healthy and strong before she met Donnie, who was off on business somewhere. Cathy couldn't figure out what her job would be when she "looked healthy" and received her assignment from the absent Donnie. She gained weight quickly, covering her thin bony frame with healthy flesh. The girls worked out every day in the fitness room—*maybe they work in gyms,* Cathy thought. But they all left for work in the evening. Rita encouraged her to work out, too, and she had fun competing with the others.

She never saw Cindy Lou again and asked the girls about her. They looked back and forth at each other and shrugged. Rita told her Donnie was looking after her, giving the other girls a warning look. At the end of the second week, Cathy was presented to Donnie. His dark hair glistened in the light; he had a diamond pinky ring, and he wore a three-piece blue, pin-striped suit. He stood from behind a massive oak desk and offered Cathy his hand.

"Come in, Cathy. I've heard a lot about you. She is lovely, Rita. You've done well to bring her here. You may be dismissed." Rita quietly shut the door behind her.

"Now, Miss Cathy, tell me about yourself. What do you like to do? And how did you get to us?"

First, Cathy asked if she could ask him a question; she wanted to know what had happened to Cindy Lou. He told her he'd had to take her to a long-term care facility because she'd gotten very sick, then he asked Cathy to tell him about herself. She told him she had been a student at a fine school in Massachusetts, but she preferred not to reveal the name. She admitted she'd run away from home. Her parents were wealthy, she informed him, but cold and unloving. "If it's just the same," she said, "I'd prefer to leave it at that."

"Of course. Many of us must chart our own course, Cathy, and you seem like a remarkable and independent young woman. How old are you, may I ask?"

Cathy paused and started to lie, but finally admitted she was fifteen. "Is that too young to work for you?"

"No, indeed not. In fact, you have certain...advantages. You seem to be a bright young lady. May I ask you to read for me?" He handed her a *Wall Street Journal* and smiled broadly when she read it flawlessly. He questioned her about the article and chuckled when she demonstrated she understood it. "You are perfect! Do you like people, Cathy? Like to meet new people?"

She told him she'd been in boarding school most of her life, but when she was home she entertained her father's business connections.

"That's where we will put you. Entertaining my business connections."

"Is that what all the girls do?"

"Not exactly; none of them are as bright as you. You'll be paid by the clients. When would you like to start?"

"Immediately, sir. I hope to go to college, but I can't use my name or social, or my parents will find me."

"Some of my connections can arrange to take care of that. Perhaps we should call you Shirley, Shirley Cooper. Do you like that?"

"That's fine, Mr. Caruso."

Pressing a kiss on her brow, he said, "Call me Donnie. You're one of us now." He rang for Rita and asked her to find Cathy a suitable dress for attending a play that evening, adding that she would be called Shirley from now on.

And that's how Cathy became a prostitute. She started off slowly, being an escort to dinner or a reception, or attending a cultural event on the arm of a well-heeled gentleman. She didn't find it too unpleasant in the beginning.

The other girls drew away from her, realizing she was too good for them. She was assigned to wealthy clients, and she charmed them all. One day, Rita took her to a doctor for a check-up. He examined her thoroughly, including a pelvic, and drew blood. Cathy asked Rita on the way back to the house if that was entirely necessary. "You lived on the streets, Cathy–Shirley–we must be sure you didn't contract anything. I'm sorry; it's simply what we do to keep you safe."

* * *

After her tests came back negative and Donnie learned, to his delight, that she was a virgin; he told Rita they had to prepare her for someone special. She would bring in a lot of money. He rubbed his hands gleefully. "We lucked out on this one, Rita!" Rita shook her head. "Buck up, old gal, you'll get a big bonus out of this one."

"Pick someone kind, Donnie. She's not one you can fix by putting her on drugs and getting her high."

"She's too valuable for that. Find me a few like her, and we can upgrade our services. I agree; I'll look for someone special for her first time."

Two weeks later Donnie informed Rita he had the perfect client, an elderly widower he had run into at the lounge in an expensive hotel. He'd never contracted for services before. Donnie got their doctor to give the man Viagra because his wife had been gone several years. "No other women. He'll be clean, Rita. Don't worry—and it's ten thousand dollars for a virgin. He insisted. He wants to be safe, too."

"If he hurts her, I'll hurt him—or you, Donnie."

"Send her in, and I'll talk to her."

High End Girl

Cathy came into Donnie's office wondering what was going on. She'd figured something was up. By this time, she received her assignments and went out.

"Sit, Shirley. Have you enjoyed your time with us?"

"Yes, Sir."

"Met some nice people, have you?"

"Most are okay. Some try to get a little fresh, asking for more, you know."

"When you helped your father, did you ever give a little more?" Donnie asked. Cathy didn't know he was aware of the results of her doctor's visit. She mumbled that she had not, uncomfortable.

"We have an elderly client who is willing to pay a lot more if you offer a bit more. He's a widower, and very lonely. He's only been with his wife, who died several years ago. I interviewed him carefully, and you have nothing to fear."

Cathy narrowed her eyes. "Is this expected of all the girls?"

He calmly replied, "It is."

"This 'escort service' is really a prostitution ring?"

"Now, Shirley, don't get worked up. We all know men have needs. You're a classy girl, and you'll have the best men out there."

"The best men looking for prostitutes!"

"All men look for women, Shirley. We make them pay for the privilege. Don't ever give it away. You'll make a lot of money this way. I thought you wanted to go to college."

"Thanks a lot, Donnie."

"You'll like Mr. Foster, Cathy. I had to talk him into this. He's not your average skirt-chaser. He's a lonely old man. Make him happy."

Cathy heard echoes of her father's voice. "Do it, Cathy." Maybe she'd always been a prostitute, like her mother. She shrugged. "I'll do my best."

"Talk to Rita. She can give you some pointers."

Rita did, and supplied her with lubricants to make her first experience easier. She even hugged her when she wished her luck.

Suck it up, Cathy. This is your lot in life. Families like Betsy's aren't for girls like you. Donnie himself took her in the limo and got out at the hotel. He walked in with her and introduced her to Stan Foster, her "host" for the evening. Leaning close, Donnie kissed her cheek and whispered, "Make him happy, and I'll make you rich."

Smiling brightly, Cathy slipped her arm into Mr. Foster's. Once again, her clothes and her hairstyle made her appear older. Mr. Foster suggested they start with dinner and escorted her to the dining room. She accepted a cocktail, needing all the bracing up she could get. Upstairs in his room, he disappeared into the bathroom and came out wearing an elegant pair of silk pajamas.

Excusing herself, Cathy followed, fishing out a negligée from her evening bag. Once suitably attired, she rejoined him in the living room of his suite. She thought briefly of her success with using alcohol on her father's associate, but Mr. Foster wasn't a drinker. He appeared as nervous as she, and he admitted as much. He told her he had to wait for the medicine to take effect.

Cathy wept in his arms. He was gentle as he held her and thanked her. "I've been lonely, Shirley, and you've made an old man very happy."

She liked the widower and even felt sorry for him. Every time he was in town he called for her, arranging it before he came to make sure she was available. Other customers were not as nice as he was, but Donnie was true to his word and arranged his better customers for her. Because she was classy and intelligent, they liked her and she developed a regular clientele who took her to fancy dances, events, and performances. Learning she would accompany Mr. Foster on Friday night, she looked forward to it. Often, he didn't ask for "a little more," contenting himself with sleeping beside her, cuddling her. He was a sweet person, and she became quite fond of him. That night, about two o'clock, they were roused by pounding on the door. Stanley rushed to open it. "Goodness, Charles, you'll wake the entire floor. What are you doing here?"

"What are you doing, dear old dad? The desk clerk wouldn't give me a key, even when I proved I'm your son. He said you and 'Mrs. Foster' retired early and didn't wish to be disturbed. Do you have a woman in here?"

"That's none of your business, but he's correct. I do not wish to be disturbed."

"I'm disturbed, Dad." Pushing his father aside, he strode into the bedroom, where Cathy clutched the sheets around her. He went to the bedside and jerked the covers off, revealing her nakedness. "How long has this been going on?" He looked at his father in fury. Then he turned to Cathy. "Listen to me!" he yelled. He ranted for a few minutes, calling her horrible names and threatening her. "You won't get a penny from the old man, you..." And the names continued. Cathy learned new words for what she did—and felt she deserved every one of them.

Stan Foster cried out, "Stop it, Charlie! She's a sweet girl, and she doesn't deserve this. Are you out of your mind? Drunk? High? To come in here like this and terrorize a young woman?!"

The younger man swiveled around, tearing his lust-filled eyes off Cathy. He pushed his father hard, causing him to fall against the chair.

Cathy grabbed a robe and knelt beside him. "You've knocked him out! We need to get help."

Charlie snorted and grabbed his father's tie off the dresser, looping it around his wrists and tying him to the chair. "I'm going to get what he's paid for."

Then he raped her. When she tried to scream, he slapped her and punched her. When his father stirred, he pummeled him with his fists. Breathless, he fell on Cathy again, and her tears increased his violence. When he passed out, Cathy eased out from under his powerful body and knelt beside Mr. Foster. She wiped his brow with a cool cloth until he came around. Leaning heavily on her, he got to the phone and called for help, asking the front desk personnel to get the police.

"I'm sorry, Shirley. I never expected this. You look terrible, Honey." Soon the police knocked at the door, and Cathy managed to let them in before she collapsed.

"Who did this to you?" one of the two officers demanded. The other approached Mr. Foster, but Cathy pointed to the bedroom, where they found Charles sprawled on the bed. Cathy and Mr. Foster were taken to the hospital. That night they treated and released Mr. Foster, but Cathy remained in Intensive Care with internal bleeding. The next morning, when she came around, the interrogator got the story out of her. She had her false identification in her pocketbook; when the name Shirley Cooper was run, it didn't reveal anything—but the prostitution ring was closed immediately, and soon Donnie and Rita were awaiting prosecution.

Cathy remained in the hospital for a week, and the social worker found her a place in a homeless shelter. She loved it! The staff reminded her of Betsy's family, and she attended chapel every day. When her period didn't come, she attributed it to the beating. But after she missed it for another month she told a female staff member, and they took her to a pregnancy center ministry. The test revealed she was pregnant. Donnie made all the girls use condoms with the clients to avoid diseases and pregnancy, but the one time she didn't—couldn't—use one, she got pregnant. *Some girls have all the luck.* The counselor showed her pictures of unborn babies, but she wasn't too keen on abortion and agreed she'd carry the child.

When she returned to the mission, the director sat beside her in his office. He admitted his suspicions that she wasn't 21, and she wasn't Shirley Cooper. "I want to help you, but we have custody issues. If you're a minor, as I believe, we'll get in big trouble housing you. I've spoken to a wonderful maternity home in Columbus, Ohio. They'll take you, but they must have your parents' permission. You do have parents, don't you?"

Cathy hung her head. These people had been nice to her, accepting her, praying with her, and tending to her recovering wounds, and they knew she'd been a prostitute. "My name is Catherine Walker. My parents are Evan and Audrey Walker, from Boston. I ran away almost a year ago. Do I have to see them?"

Scribbling furiously, the director took this information down. "Thank you, Catherine."

"Call me Cathy."

"Okay, Cathy. Thank you for trusting me. I'll see what we can do." After she left, he called the social worker at Hope House, who suggested he let them work with her parental issues since she'd be living with them longer. As soon as they had obtained permission, Cathy would come to Columbus.

Cathy's father refused to take time off to travel to Wheeling but gave his permission, granting Hope House custody via fax. Her mother called and begged to speak to her, but Cathy didn't want to take the call. She was ashamed. To the delight of the shelter staff, the Hope House housemother had a daughter who lived in Wheeling and visited her mother often, and she agreed to take Cathy with her. She pulled up in front of the mission Friday afternoon and leaned across the seat to push the door open. Cathy was relieved the woman knew nothing of her past, and found her warm and kindly.

"I lived on the streets for a while, but I've been tested and I don't have anything contagious."

"I hear you're pregnant, and I know *that's* not contagious!" They laughed.

Cathy began to relax about her move—if the housemother was anything like her daughter, she must be nice.

"Mom loves her girls, Cathy. You'll feel right at home."

"I felt at home in the mission for the first time in my life—except once when I visited my dorm advisor over a school break."

Jennifer cut her eyes over to Cathy.

"I ran away from home about thirteen months ago."

"Wow, that bad, huh?"

"Yep." Cathy fell silent, and Jennifer didn't pry. Instead, they talked about her nieces, nephews, and students—she was a teacher.

"You'll love Hope House. It's in the historical district, and it's a beautiful home. Mom's happy there. She's a widow, and she has a job that suits her to a T. She's loving and good-natured. You'll like her, I promise."

Cathy wondered. Her last housemother had recruited her for a prostitution ring. *Creeps.*

When they pulled up in front of the elegant mansion, Cathy thought again of her parents' house. She followed Jennifer up the steps, but before they could ring the bell, the door swung open. Even before embracing her daughter, Ginny pulled Cathy into her arms, welcoming her warmly. Tears sprung to the teen's eyes as she remembered Betsy's mother—this woman felt like her, and she felt warmed. She found herself smiling at the two women as they hugged.

"Now," Ginny said briskly, "Have you eaten? Knowing Jennifer, she didn't stop. Are you starving?"

"Mom's answer for anything is food," Jennifer said.

"She looks like she could use a few pounds. I understand you were in the hospital? Are you well?" Ginny asked.

"Nothing contagious. I was...beaten up pretty badly."

"Oh, Honey, I'm sorry. Anything broken?"

"I had internal bleeding—ended up losing my spleen."

Jennifer was horrified. "Who did that to you?!"

Cathy simply shook her head, unable to talk about it yet. Ginny touched her daughter's arm, an unspoken signal that this was best left to the professionals. Jennifer fought tears and changed the subject, asking her mother what she had to eat.

"We had meat loaf and mashed potatoes with green beans. I made extra to have enough for you. Cathy, do you want to meet the girls before you eat?" Ginny steered her to the living room, where four girls in various stages of pregnancy looked up to say hi.

Jennifer and Cathy devoured the leftovers, but Cathy was quiet while Ginny and Jennifer talked. Ginny looked over at her and asked if she felt tired.

"Yes, Ma'am. I don't know why; I didn't do that much today."

"Fatigue is a symptom of early pregnancy. Let's get you settled in bed. The others will go to school tomorrow, but you'll stay home and talk to our social worker so we can plan out your course."

"Thank you, Ma'am." Ginny and her daughter exchanged looks; this was a special girl.

Ginny settled Cathy in a two-person room. "We'll have a roommate for you next week, but for now, are you all right by yourself?"

"Yes, Ma'am. I had a room to myself for months."

"Your towels are on the bed. Hang them on the towel rack on the back of your closet door. You're first, so choose your closet and bed. Need anything else?"

Candy tried to suppress a huge yawn and shook her head.

Ginny hugged her. "Welcome, Cathy. We're glad to have you at Hope House."

Cathy gave her a sad smile and thanked her. She washed her face, brushed her teeth quickly, and was asleep in fifteen minutes.

Hope House

Cathy felt the sun on her face before she opened her eyes. She stretched and looked around. She'd hardly noticed the room the night before, but it was cheerful, with yellow curtains and matching bedspreads. At the end of each bed stood a desk facing the wall, with shelves above it. A long dresser separated the two beds, and beyond each desk was a closet, obviously added after the room was built. Cathy looked for her jeans and found them folded neatly on the desk chair. Someone had come in and closed the curtains as well.

Her stomach growled, and Cathy dreaded the wait for lunch. At Donnie's, if you were late for a meal you waited until the next one. At the time, she was grateful to have regular food. *Oh, well.* She peeked into the hall, looking one way then the other, and scooted across to the bathroom. Once dressed, she crept down the stairs. Miss Ginny entered the foyer and looked up.

"I thought I heard you up there. Are you hungry? I'm glad you slept in. You needed it." Ginny stretched out her hand. "Are you a big breakfast eater? Eggs and bacon or cereal?"

A towering door off the foyer swung open, and a smiling young woman crossed the distance to take Cathy's hand. "You must be Cathy. I'm Beth, the social worker. We've been looking forward to having you with us. Welcome."

"Join us for a cup of coffee, Beth?"

"I'm ready for another cup. Just getting up, Cathy?"

Cathy flushed. "I'm sorry I overslept."

Beth tucked the girl's hand under her arm. "Nonsense! Ginny told me you were worn out last night, and you needed some rest. We're used to pregnant girls around here." As they talked, they walked back to the airy, spacious kitchen and sat at a round oak table.

Ginny went to the stove, asking over her shoulder, "Scrambled or fried?"

"Uh, I can wait for lunch if it's too much trouble."

"Thin as you are? I think not! Let's feed the baby," Ginny replied with a smile.

"Scrambled." Cathy felt dizzy with the love swirling around her. The girl who'd never felt love until Betsy's mother embraced her was overcome by the love in Beth's touch and Ginny's smile. *What is it about them that feels like Betsy's family?*

"We understand you've come to us down a tough road. Feel like talking about it?"

"Give her some time to wake up," Ginny chided.

"What have you heard?" Cathy asked, wondering if they knew she'd been a prostitute.

"We heard you were discharged from the hospital after being beaten severely and stayed in a mission until your parents gave us custody. You're sixteen?" Beth asked.

"Almost. I'll be sixteen in September."

"You look very mature for sixteen," Ginny said, putting a steaming plate of eggs and bacon in front of her.

Cathy looked down, avoiding eye contact. She shoveled a forkful of eggs into her mouth. Beth and Ginny exchanged glances; they wouldn't correct her and insist on grace this meal. Cathy reached for the glass of orange juice as soon as Ginny placed it in front of her.

"Thanks! Delicious."

"You're quite welcome, Sweetie," Ginny said, adding, "I did feed her when she came in last night."

"Knowing you, I'm sure you did. Where's Jennifer?"

"Off to see her sister."

Cathy hardly said two words during her meal and gave only the minimal responses during her intake interview. She did communicate that she'd grown up in boarding schools. Beth gathered she felt no love from her parents and was left alone most of her life. She had heard lots of sad stories at Hope House, but this girl touched her heart; Beth hoped the home lived up to its name for her. They didn't touch on her months as a prostitute. Beth let it go, preferring to develop a level of trust where Cathy would confide that on her own. Cathy told the social worker her goal was college, though she wasn't sure of her major. Beth said she was sure Cathy had the intelligence, but she hadn't completed high school. In a three-way conference with Ginny and the psychologist who worked with the girls, they'd develop some options and let her choose. Seeing Cathy was fading fast, Beth suggested a nap.

"I can do my chores," Cathy replied.

"You'll have those assigned, but you've been through a lot. First, I want you evaluated by a physician to see what you can do and what you must not do. She's sent for your medical records, and we have an appointment for you on Monday. This is Friday. Take the weekend to get to know the girls. Take it easy, and we'll worry about the rest later."

* * *

Beth went into the kitchen to tell Ginny that Cathy went upstairs to take a nap, and Ginny asked if she wanted a sandwich. "No, thanks," Beth responded.

"What do you think of our gal?"

"You first."

Tears glistened in Ginny's eyes. "I've heard many sad stories here, but she seems too quiet. I'd say she's depressed."

Beth huffed. "I'd say she had the right. She never mentioned her months as a prostitute. Imagine, a fifteen-year-old girl being sold like that! I didn't let on that we knew, because I want her to tell us. She's very intelligent and wants to go to college." Beth took a deep breath. "I want John's assessment on this."

Ginny agreed. John, the psychologist who ran group therapy every Thursday night, often weighed in on case management for the girls. "I thought we'd let her settle in. I have an appointment for her with Dr. Waggoner on Monday."

"You told me. That's wise. She has the hospital records; Cathy well may be put on restricted activity." Beth went through the status of each of the girls and found them to be right on course. "We have a pleasant group right now, and everyone is doing well."

"We're all set then?"

"For once, we have no major drama. It'll be a good space for Cathy." Beth stood. "I'll head out and have a nice long time with my baby before the kids get home."

"I'll see you Monday, then. Come in later; our appointment at the doctor is at nine."

Cathy spent much of the weekend resting. She got along fine with the other girls. She was used to the girls at Donnie's; many of them were not very bright. At least these girls were clean. *No drugs in this place*, she thought. Cathy had come to realize Donnie supplied the girls with drugs to keep them placid. She had always refused his offers, and because she was his high-end girl, he hadn't pushed it. When she went upstairs to lie down, the girls came into the kitchen to report to Ginny. Cathy was taking another nap, but they vowed they'd been nice to her.

Ginny explained that Cathy had required major surgery before coming to Hope House, and she was still recovering. When they questioned her further, she reminded them of the rules: no gossip, and if a girl wanted to share, she must do it herself.

Sunday morning, the girls climbed in the van for church and Cathy shared about the 'cool' chapel services at the Mission. She was thoughtful and attentive in the service, although she didn't join in the singing. She didn't know the songs.

On Monday, the doctor's appointment was prolonged when the physical exam revealed a swollen and painful kidney. After scans, the doctor thought it was bruised, not bleeding, but it would be sore awhile. She told Ginny the girl had been terribly beaten, and she was amazed by her level of pain toler-ance. "Perhaps she's depressed—God knows, who wouldn't be? —but some low-level pain meds will help her. Let her sleep a lot. She hasn't threatened to harm herself, has she?"

"No indication of that. She wants to take care of the baby. Will this damage the child?"

"No. Her injuries all occurred the night she was raped; the pregnancy need to urinate will be difficult for a few weeks. I want to see her back in two weeks to evaluate the kidney function. Make sure she drinks a lot of water. Is she peeing okay?"

"I'll ask her and keep an eye on it," Ginny said.

"She's getting dressed. I'll go check on her." The doctor left the room, and Ginny bowed her head to pray for the umpteenth time for this child-mother who had been horribly abused.

Cathy joined Miss Ginny in the doctor's office. "Ready to go?" she asked, with her sad little smile.

Ginny reached into her purse for her keys. "Yep, let's go. You want to grab a sandwich or a shake somewhere?"

"Don't we need to be back for the others when they get in from school? No school for me, by the way, until after my next appointment."

"Dr. Waggoner explained you have a bruised kidney as well as your surgery recovery."

"Yeah."

"A lot of pain?"

"A little. She gave me some tablets, but I don't do drugs. Never have. Never will."

"She said it was a mild prescription. Taking something for pain is not doing drugs."

"Lots of drugs on the streets are prescription, Miss Ginny."

"Can you use the bathroom? She said I was to be sure you drink a lot of water and pee."

"That hurts some, yeah, but I can do it."

Blinking back tears, Ginny joked, "You're peeing for two, you know."

Cathy's hand dropped to her tummy. "I know. She said the baby's okay. I didn't hurt the baby. I got beat up before I even knew—I got pregnant the night I was raped. She did STD screening, too."

"That's good. We do that with every girl who comes into Hope House." Ginny looked at her watch. "The bus drops the girls off at three. We have plenty of time to stop at Chick-fil-A." Ginny called Beth from the restaurant so that she wouldn't wait for them. After they ate, Ginny asked if Cathy needed any clothes.

"The police let me go in the...place where I stayed and I got my stuff. I'm okay."

Cathy remained at Hope House with Miss Ginny and Beth, who came in every morning. John told her he felt good about the doctor's advice to keep her close to home and defer any activities until she was further along in her physical recovery. She was depressed, but John thanked God, once again, that the mother's concern for her child enabled her to walk through some serious stuff. Women, even child-women, were amazing creatures.

Cathy didn't talk much but appeared more relaxed. She even joined in some horseplay one evening, but when one of the girls hit her in the back with a pillow, she sank to the floor, groaning. Another ran to find Ginny, and they helped her up.

"I'm fine," Cathy assured them through her tears. "You didn't hurt me, Lexie."

"I did! Look at you. What's wrong?"

Hearing the commotion, Miss Ginny came. "Cathy has a bruised kidney, girls. She'll be fine, but it's sore."

"Bruised kidney? How do you bruise a kidney?" another girl asked.

"You don't," Cathy answered. "Someone else does, when he beats you to a bloody pulp."

The girls stared. "Why?" Amy asked. "Did he rob you?"

"No. He was a spoiled rich brat, and he didn't like it that I loved his father, and his father loved me. He thought I was after the old man's money." Seeing no more information would be forthcoming, the girls hugged Cathy and asked if she wanted to go upstairs. When she wanted to stay, they settled her on the couch and picked out a movie to watch.

Lexie give Cathy a quick, gentle hug when they parted outside her room. "I'm sorry I hurt you."

Cathy's first real smile flashed when she hugged the girl back. "It's okay, Lexie. You didn't mean to. I feel better now. No big deal."

When Beth came in the following morning, she found Cathy at a late breakfast in the kitchen. She pulled up a chair and took the cup of coffee Ginny offered. "Feeling better today, Cathy?"

"We had a bit of a setback last night when the girls were playing around. One of them accidently hit her in the back with a pillow. But she wouldn't even take a Tylenol, Beth."

"Miss Ginny, it's fine. No big deal."

"Sometimes I wonder if we shouldn't let up on the no gossip rule—at least when someone has an injury," Ginny said. Glancing at Cathy, Ginny continued. "Cathy told us last night the man who 'beat her to a bloody pulp' was the son of an old man she loved. He was afraid she was after his father's money."

"He raped me, too. He's the father of the baby. That won't make the baby come out mental, will it? You know, bad genes or something?"

Beth took a deep breath. "No. You are what you are surrounded by when you're a baby." She studied Cathy, finally asking, "How did you know the old man?"

"He was a…a client." She hung her head, whispering, "I was a prostitute. But the old man didn't ask for much. We did it sometimes, but mostly he wanted to cuddle and hold me. We hadn't done it in a while. I know it was his son who got me pregnant. He didn't use a condom, and he raped me several times that night. He beat up his father, too. When he passed out, I put a cold cloth on the old man's head and roused him. He called for help. The cops cuffed his son and took us to the hospital. I was rolled out of there on a stretcher and had surgery early the next morning: ruptured spleen."

Beth knelt in front of Cathy's chair and took both her hands. "You're a survivor, you know."

"I'm a prostitute," Cathy sobbed.

Beth gathered her in her arms. "Did you know Jesus loved prostitutes? He said they are closer to the Kingdom of God than religious folks."

"He doesn't want me in His Kingdom."

"Oh, but He does," Ginny protested. "He loves you. He came all the way from Heaven to find you, Cathy. If you let Him, He will pick you up in His arms, His little lost lamb, and carry you to His Father's house."

"Nobody wants me. My own parents never wanted me! The old man was the only person who ever wanted me, and he paid for it."

"God wants you, Cathy. Jesus left heaven and came looking for you. He's standing here now, ready to give you everlasting love. He'll wash your sins away and make all things new. When you give Him your heart, He makes you into a new creation."

In the Hope House kitchen, still in her pajamas, Cathy yielded her heart to God. Even the two women who ministered to her felt the presence of God in that place. With glad tears, they welcomed their new little sister into the family of God.

"I feel good!"

"It is a wonderful feeling to be born again."

"No. Well, yes. That too, but my back doesn't hurt anymore. All the pain is gone."

The next morning, the doctor confirmed Cathy had no swelling. Furthermore, her surgical incision had all but disappeared. She shook her head as she looked at Ginny, who was sitting beside Cathy, holding her hand. After explaining her findings, she added, "You folks at Hope House have something going with the man upstairs. I need you praying for all my patients. Let's keep her home until her regular pregnancy visit, and make education plans at that time. You're good to go, Miss Cathy."

Cathy skipped out of the doctor's office. Ginny loved to see the girl's new, happy countenance, and grinned. "I told you God loves you. He healed you, Cathy."

She stopped and stared. "He did, didn't He? Thank You, Jesus. This is like the Bible, isn't it, Miss Ginny?"

"It is. You're a miracle."

"Let's go tell Beth!"

At Hope House, laughing and crying, Cathy informed Beth of her spontaneous recovery. John, who had stopped by to confer with them, joined the celebration. He hugged the teenager. Considering his warm brown eyes, Cathy realized he loved her, too.

"I felt it when I came here, but I didn't know what it was. Once I visited my dorm counselor's home, and I felt it there. They took me to church; it was the first time I'd ever been in a church. It's God's love. In them. In you guys. Wow!"

John beamed. "Right you are, Cathy, and it's in your eyes, too. You'll comfort others with the comfort you have received."

"Really? Because I want to. I want to help others. I want to be a social worker, like Beth, and help lots of girls."

"That's a good goal," John encouraged. "We need to have you evaluated. We all know you're intelligent, but we need to see where you are education-ally so we can plan the next step for you."

"Let's go to the kitchen," Ginny suggested. "I can fix us some sand-wiches, and we can talk about it."

"Miss Jennifer said her mom's remedy for everything is food." Cathy giggled, and the adults blinked back tears at the happy sound typical to teenage girls, which they'd never heard from this one before.

"I'm all for one of Miss Ginny's sandwiches," John enthused, and the happy group headed for the round oak table.

Cathy stood beside Ginny spreading the mayo while Ginny piled up lettuce, tomato, and slices of last night's pot roast. The new Christian insisted on saying the blessing, and poured out her thanksgiving and praises to the God who makes all things new.

"I know I can be a good mother now, Beth."

"You have a lot of time to think about it, but it's your decision, and we'll stand beside you and make it happen."

"I want to keep this baby. He's mine, and he'll love me."

"What's not to love, Cathy?" John said, squeezing her hand. Again, Cathy felt their love surrounding her.

"Okay, let's consider the options. First, John, I don't think Cathy needs to be in a regular high school—unless you want to be. She completed her freshman year of high school, but she's been through too much, seen too much of the harsh side of life. She's way more mature than your average teenager."

John nodded, but turned to Cathy for confirmation. She shrugged her shoulders. "Who knows better than you, Cathy? What do you want to do?

"I don't know my options."

"Fair enough; we really don't either," Beth admitted. "First we need an educational assessment, which we can get through the school system, over at adult Ed. We'll get you tested and go from there. How about that?"

"Good plan. This meeting is adjourned until further information is obtained," John said. "Cathy, I heard you asked Jesus to be the Lord of your life, and I see it with my own two eyes. Good for you."

She beamed. "I feel good, inside and out."

John extended his arm, and she slipped under it for a hug. "See you Sunday. Church will mean more to you this week."

She found this to be true. She moved forward to the altar at the close of the service and once again felt God's love swirl around her when the pastor and others laid their hands on her.

New Arrivals

A new girl, Laura, replaced one of the departing girls. Laura was a cheerleader from a high school in Morgantown, West Virginia, and looked every bit of it. She had long, blonde, bouncy hair, and usually wore it in a pony tail. She was pretty, enthusiastic, and outgoing. Her boyfriend supported her plan to adopt. He was recruited for the University of West Virginia football team and knew he wasn't ready to parent. Laura's main concern was being out of cheerleading—she might lose her scholarship opportunities. All the girls were jealous of her regular letters and calls from Sam. She started attending the local high school.

Another girl decided to place her baby. She wanted to be a legal secretary, and after completing high school in May, she'd enroll in a course at the community college. The father of her child waned nothing to do with the baby and signed the surrender papers immediately. Her family had several younger children and could offer no support; she'd realized she would struggle alone. After meeting a set of adoptive parents, she agreed to surrender the little girl to a well-established couple who could provide her with advantages and a stable home.

By this time, Cathy was enrolled part-time in GED classes and working at a nearby pizza restaurant. Beth was supporting her goals to attend college. She was bright enough to attend the community college, but she had to earn a GED to enroll. Although peaceful with her decision to follow Christ and pleasant to the girls around her, she kept to herself. She felt everyone was better than she was, but Candy's arrival in March drew her out of her shell.

She was horrified when she learned her seventeen-year old new friend had been sexually abused by her mother's boyfriend since she was thirteen. They bonded over their feelings of abuse and the degradation they had experienced. Often Ginny saw them sitting cross-legged on their beds, discussing the men who had used them without conscience.

Candy's mother's boyfriend claimed she had seduced him, although he had raped her continually and she begged him to leave her alone. When her mother discovered Candy was pregnant and she named her mother's boyfriend as the father, the woman slapped her and threw her out. Her high school counselor helped her get to Hope House.

Cathy told Candy her father encouraged her to use her sexuality to entertain his business associates and confided in her new friend about her months as a prostitute. They both agreed men were scum—except for John, and Beth's husband Tom—and they both wanted to keep their babies. John and Beth knew the girls who were rejected wanted someone who belonged to them, who would love them unconditionally. Often the most unqualified girls were the ones who desperately longed for their babies. Beth had all the girls work through workbooks on single parenting and adoption, trying to challenge them with the difficulties of single parenting. Cathy grieved for the life she was choosing for her baby and longed for him to have two committed parents in his family—whatever that was—but she wanted him. Candy wanted her baby, too, and only gave lip service to adoption.

Lexie gave birth to her son in May. Beth found a college with a cafeteria management program and a daycare to take the baby while Lexie completed the two-year course. The program had an excellent placement rate once the girls completed the program.

Michelle replaced Lexie. *Talk about opposites!* Cathy thought. Michelle had attended an elite private boarding school like Cathy—but she flourished there, competing in academic events and studying hard. She also had an emotionally distant father, but Michelle compensated by excelling academically and bringing numerous trophies to her school. She wore thick glasses and paid little attention to her appearance beyond wearing designer clothing. No wonder some boy took advantage of her, turning her head with declarations of love that disappeared when she became pregnant. Of course, then he wanted nothing to do with her or the baby.

Michelle came to Hope House convinced she'd place her baby in a good home and go on to college, maybe even graduate school She had the brains to earn her way. Her parents, despite being Catholic, were angry she didn't abort the baby. Michelle, who was actively involved in her church and attended pro-life rallies, knew she couldn't live with killing an unborn child.

Beth and Ginny hoped Cathy would bond because of their similar backgrounds, but Michelle made Cathy feel inferior. She had made good choices, except for the bum she trusted, and Cathy felt even worse about herself. She buried herself in work at the restaurant, determined to make money for her own education. Sometimes peer pressure was a good thing, but this time it backfired; Cathy withdrew from socializing with the other girls. She longed to share her new faith, but Laura was a nominal Christian, Candy had never experienced any religious training, and Michelle was a devout Catholic. They dropped her off at her church on their way to the church that supported the home, where the staff attended.

Ginny approached her after work Saturday. "We are hoping to receive a Christian young lady soon, Cathy. I hope you'll find a good friend."

"I like the girls, Miss Ginny."

"You've always been kind...; I think Missy will be a good match for you. I spoke to her pastor, and she sounds like a real sweetheart. Laura and Michelle will be attending summer school to catch up the course work they missed this spring, so we'll put them in the same room. Candy will share a room with a new girl the court is sending us; her name is Myra."

Cathy shrugged. "Whatever."

"Did you have a good evening at work?"

The teenager brightened. "Friday night means good tips." She reached into her pocket and handed over a fistful of bills. "Would you deposit this for me?"

"You've done well! This must be over sixty dollars!"

"Seventy-two dollars and eighty-five cents. I don't know if my father will help with college at all. He and Mother don't seem to be getting along. I bet they're headed for divorce."

"I'm sorry," Ginny consoled.

Cathy shrugged. "They didn't have much of a marriage. When I visited my dorm advisor, her mom and dad loved each other. You could tell by the way they looked at each other and laughed together. They held hands in church and slept in the same bedroom, even shared a bed."

"Which is as it should be. My husband was in the military and had to be gone on deployments for months, or sometimes even a year. When he was home, he looked forward to being in our bed. Sometimes the kids would pile in with us."

"How many kids did you have?"

"Five. Jennifer is the middle child: the only one who never married."

"How many grandchildren? I know the four who go to our church."

"My younger son will bring his three boys this summer. My oldest daughter has two girls, thirteen and fifteen, and an older boy who is stationed in San Diego. I plan to fly out there in a few months."

"Okay, I think I counted right: four plus three, plus two...and how many in California?"

"Two boys in college. Eleven in all."

"Wow!"

"I'm blessed with a fine family, and all you wonderful girls who enrich my life."

"Sometimes we're pains, Miss Ginny, but you're good to us anyway. When will this Missy be here?"

"She needs to come; she's close to her mother and brother, and she's finding it hard to leave. She has a job at MacDonald's, and the family's poor, so she's trying to work as long as she can. By the way, your father sent another check today. I gather you don't speak with him?"

"No, Ma'am. He's always wanted me out of the house, out of his way. I'd rather be poor and have a mother and brother I love, like Missy. I'll start praying for her now."

Missy Arrives

Missy arrived at Hope House in July. To keep Cathy's spirits up, Ginny stretched the no gossip rule to tell her she'd talked to Missy's pastor. She told Cathy some of the things he'd said about her, and Cathy felt a connection, curiosity, and growing excitement. The day she arrived, Cathy had completed her chores and was upstairs in the bedroom she'd share with the new girl. Miss Ginny sat on the front porch to wait for the O'Malley family, and Cathy heard them talking. She heard the door to Beth's office open, then close a moment later. The family started up the stairs, and Cathy went out to the hallway to see them: two small, brown-skinned females and a tall, broad-shouldered redhead who had to be the brother. *Boy, they sure don't look alike; maybe he was adopted. But he is cute!* she thought.

"Hi, Missy, I'm Cathy, your roommate. I'm glad you're here. We've been praying for you."

Missy's black eyes shone and her sad face curved into a smile. "Hi, Cathy. This is my mom, Alice O'Malley, and my brother, Jimmy."

Jimmy lugged her suitcase without any effort. When he beamed at Cathy, she literally felt her tummy turn over. *Wow, if I could find a guy like that,* she thought, but immediately remembered nice guys didn't like girls like her; she remembered how he'd stared up at her belly when he was climbing the stairs.

"Come on, I'll show you the room." Cathy took Missy's hand and practically dragged her to the room closest the stairs. She pointed out the other girls' rooms, and Miss Ginny's suite at the end of the hall. Jimmy threw the suitcase on his sister's bed and chatted with the girls while Missy put her clothes and things in the drawers. She placed a photo of him and her mother on her desk.

The room was warm and comfortable. Twin beds hugged the side walls, and in the middle of the back wall, a wide window framed with cheerful yellow curtains allowed the eastern sunlight to flood into the room. The matching bedspreads gave the room a cozy feel. Two desks faced the wall at the foot of each bed, with shelves above them for books and knick-knacks.

Cathy presented Missy with a stuffed kitty she had made for her, and Missy wanted to show it to her mom. Ginny had taken her to see the other rooms, so Missy called down the hall for her mother.

"Look, Mom. See what Cathy made me," Missy shoved the soft little kitty into Alice's hands. "Isn't that cute? She made it, and she said she'd teach me how to make them, too."

"Why, Cathy, how thoughtful! What a nice thing to do. Thank you, Honey." Alice put her arm around Cathy and gave her a hug.

I'd rather have this mom—but I don't want Jimmy for a brother! Cathy's spirits lifted. She was going to love this new roommate.

Missy had a terrible time saying good-bye to her family. She clung to her mother and said it was hard to let her go. Her big brother picked her off the floor, promising to come see her. Miss Ginny tried to make the parting easier by telling her all the things they had to do. Cathy watched Missy take a deep breath, smile tremulously, and draw from some inner reserve to send them on their way.

To offer further distraction, Cathy suggested they go meet the two girls who were home at the time: Myra and Candy. Big mistake. Mouthy, mean Myra was rude and hurtful. Candy, who wasn't a bad sort but was strongly influenced by her roommate, was kind until Myra shut her down. Cathy didn't exhibit Christian behavior, calling Myra a name, and immediately felt she'd blown it with her new roommate. She went to the kitchen and compounded her mistake by blurting out what happened.

"Tattling again, Miss Righteous One?" Myra taunted.

Cathy was thrown back to Donnie's house and the rough girls she'd lived with there. She clenched her fists in a defensive posture. The fist fight fizzled when Ginny diverted both girls, and when Michelle and Laura burst through the door with their test scores, Missy looked genuinely relieved. Cathy had seen Missy's horrified face, and apologized for ruining her room-mate's first day.

The snacks Ginny planned to serve were set aside when Michelle drew the housemother's attention to Laura's swollen ankles. Ginny insisted the teen lie down, and promised to bring her cookies and milk to the living room. Myra made a snide comment about exceptions to the rules, and Ginny reminded her of the times when she brought Myra tea when she was nauseated. The angry teen shrugged but remained quiet after that.

Cathy ran upstairs; returning with pillows for Laura's feet, she helped her elevate them. She glanced covertly at Missy to see how she was holding up; this was quite a beginning for her. When Ginny thanked Cathy, she shrugged off the praise, confessing that she'd called Myra a name and messed up her witness. Ginny suggested she apologize, and she protested but agreed, and excused herself.

When Missy came upstairs to finish settling in, she told Cathy she'd gotten to know Michelle and Laura a little bit. She thought plain Michelle had looked almost pretty when Ginny had hugged her and praised her grade. "The girl must come from money," Missy said, "because she's wearing a matched designer outfit." She had seen the brand in a store once, and the jeans alone cost over a hundred dollars.

"Michelle is quiet and sad looking, but doesn't that come with the turf around here, Cathy? Laura doesn't appear too sad, and she defended you because Myra was difficult," Missy told her roommate.

A teary Cathy asked her where the passage about doing what you don't want to do was, and Missy showed her Romans 8, explaining how the old nature battles our new nature. Then she showed her Romans 12, and Paul's exhortation to present our bodies a living sacrifice. They prayed together before Ginny tapped on the door asking Missy if she'd mind helping Michelle set the table, since Laura shouldn't be on her feet.

Neither Ginny nor Missy was surprised on Monday when the doctor told Laura she'd missed her due date, and the sonogram pointed to a September baby. Cathy, who thought she'd have her baby first, wasn't happy—but she wasn't at all sure about her own plans and Laura had picked out her baby's adoptive parents.

From the time Missy hit the place, Hope House seemed to revolve around her and the God she adored. Cathy felt loved and accepted, even admitting to her roommate that she'd been a prostitute. They both agonized over their decision about their babies.

"What's better for my baby and my family?" Missy thought aloud, explaining her brother was in trade school and her mother was taking classes to get her RN license. She told Cathy about their father's abandonment and their struggles since.

"But he's mine," Cathy defended her choice. "I don't care that his father was a rapist. I can't let him go!"

Missy said her baby was a child of rape too, and she felt the same way. "I love my little girl, but I have to think about what God wants, not what I want." Cathy teased her about thinking her baby was a girl when they hadn't done a sonogram yet, but when they confirmed it, she wasn't surprised. God seemed to tell Missy things.

One night after they had prayed and discussed scripture, Cathy thanked her for her help once again. "I heard Laura tell Miss Ginny she thought God brought you here to help her, but I think He brought you here to help me."

Missy laughed and asked Cathy if she thought they could both help Michelle improve her appearance. "You do great with your make-up and hair, Cathy. Can you help? Do you know the colors and what clothes go with body types? You know, fashion and all that?"

"Candy's going to beauty school when she gets through her GED, and she cut Myra's hair—it looks awful, but it was exactly what she wanted. She cut Laura's hair, too, and you know how particular she is—it takes her all the hot water and hours to get ready every day!"

"If Candy's good, why doesn't she do something with those awful roots? I'm sorry, I shouldn't have said that! I'm horrible," Missy said.

"It's the truth! But she doesn't have two nickels to rub together."

The plan went into overdrive; by the next weekend, Michelle's mother had sent her enough money to go to a private salon, and she made Candy go with her. They had a fabulous time at the mall afterward, picking out some new clothes. Missy was content with the hand-me downs in the clothing closet, donations for the House, but Michelle insisted her clothing allowance was more than she needed, and she bought Candy two nice outfits. Although Myra acted out—running off and smoking—the rest of them had a wonderful time. Miss Ginny took the rebellious teen back to Hope House, but despite Ginny's best efforts, the next week, Myra ran away. The girls and the staff identified her in a grainy photo taken at the bus station, but she was never found. For many years, they would regret not trying to be friendlier to the lost girl.

At the mall, Beth and her husband spent the remainder of the afternoon with the girls. They played with their boys and cooed over the couple's baby girl. Beth's husband was a nice guy, they agreed—not like the males they'd encountered in their lives.

Missy liked Michelle; her influence helped Cathy be less defensive, so she drew closer to Michelle, too. Michelle's aloofness faded when she felt comfortable with the others. The makeover did wonders for their friends, but Michelle's smiles did even more to make her pretty. She got contact lenses to replace her glasses, and people hardly recognized the new Michelle. One night when Michelle was doing dishes, Missy convinced Cathy to short-sheet her bed. They ran into her room, did the deed, and slipped out to hide in their room. When Michelle closed her door, they hovered in the hall, waiting for her reaction. They put their hands over their mouths to stifle their giggles, failing miserably as Michelle discovered what they'd done, yelling, "Hey! Who messed with my bed?" Ginny stood shaking her head with her hands on her hips in disapproval after she learned the prank, but gales of laughter pealed out of the room.

"Of course you can't get your feet in the bed," Laura screamed. "The joke is on you."

The door banged open and Michelle caught her friends laughing. Her dark eyes danced and she hugged them. Ginny relaxed, smiling as well, but insisted Cathy and Missy fix it. "Go in there and make up her bed, *correctly*, right now!"

The giggling twosome joined Laura, fixing up the bed, and Ginny asked Michelle if she was upset.

"No, Ma'am—I like it. Nobody's ever played with me before. I had to be perfect for my father, and all I did was study. I feel like I have friends for the first time in my life."

"You do, Sweetie. Missy loves you."

"Missy loves everybody, Miss Ginny, but I love her, too."

"Don't we all?" Ginny replied as the girls bounced into the hall, announcing Michelle's bed had been restored.

"And I didn't even put a frog in it—that's what Jimmy used to do to me," Missy added.

"That would *not* be funny! I'd die if I found an ugly, slimy old frog in my bed!"

"'Chelle, you're such a city girl! You need to come see me in the mountains when all this is behind us." Missy threw her arms around her friend's neck. "I love you!"

Michelle blinked back tears. "I love you, too. Thanks for being my friend."

"I have a feeling we'll be friends forever." Missy swept her arm in a circle to include Laura, Cathy, and Candy, who'd joined in the fun. "We've been through so much together."

"You led me to Christ, Missy. I'll never forget you," Candy said.

"All right, girls, tomorrow's church day. Go on to bed now."

"Yeah, go on with ya now," Missy echoed with an Irish lilt, skipping down the hall.

Missy had hit the place like a cascade of love. Only Myra refused to succumb to the power of God's love that Missy showed, but Missy had been afraid of Myra. Her departure wasn't mourned by anyone except Ginny, whose heart broke for the bitter girl and her unborn child. But Michelle laughed, Cathy prayed and prayed—how that girl prayed—and Candy found hope. When Laura went into labor, she woke Missy and clung to her hand, begging her to go with her to the hospital.

"I'll be next, Missy," Cathy said when her roommate returned from the hospital. "Will you come with me?"

"Wild horses couldn't keep me away, Cath! You know I will."

A New Relationship

Beth's been talking to my mom," Cathy told her roommate. "She's written and wants to come see me. I've written her back, but I haven't invited her. After Pastor's message on the unjust steward and John's discussion of forgiveness, I need to call her. Dad divorced her; she's living in Belpre, Ohio now. It's not too far."

"You should. Girls need their moms. Maybe she made some mistakes..." seeing Cathy's expression, Missy added, "Okay, a *lot* of mistakes, but she's your mother, right? And she's alone. Give her a chance."

"Pray for me, Missy. I don't even know why she moved nearby. She was always too busy trying to please my father to take any notice of me."

Missy scooted across the space between the beds and took her friend's hand. Cathy clung to it. "We don't know everything. She had her reasons." And Missy prayed for Cathy's mother.

An image of her mother's perpetually anxious face as she sought to soothe her husband's anger flashed in Cathy's mind. "She lived in a constant state of...fear, almost terror sometimes. They weren't affectionate, more like strangers living together in separate bedrooms. He used to go into her room sometimes, usually after he'd had a few drinks."

"She didn't have a lot of love, sounds like."

"I guess not. He ruled her with an iron hand. She was his puppet."

Missy returned to her prayer and asked for an anointing of love for Cathy, and the grace to forgive. "Make this a new beginning for them," she finished. Afterward, she took Cathy in her arms and held her.

The next weekend, Audrey came to Hope House. Ginny put her in Candy's bed, in the room with her daughter, and moved Candy in with Missy. Cathy begged to stay with her prayer partner, but John and Ginny agreed she needed to be with her mother. The two of them met with Beth Friday afternoon, and John came in Saturday to counsel with them.

Audrey was awkward with the girls at first, but they all had fun and laughed and talked through dinner Friday night. They teased Miss Ginny about her one culinary disaster, a failed bread pudding, and told her Missy made better bread. Ginny laughingly agreed, saying she'd never made bread until Missy taught her. Missy claimed she'd had to go to the grocery with her to show her where to find the yeast! Candy and Michelle described their makeovers and day at the mall. They all fell apart laughing when Candy declared she didn't know what to do without her boobs hanging out.

"She looks pretty, doesn't she, Miss Audrey?" Missy asked.

"That guy in the GED class, Joe—he stares at her," Laura teased.

"Yeah, and they have lunch together," Michelle added.

"Cut it out, guys!" Candy blushed.

Smiling, Audrey reached out to touch Candy's face. "You're very pretty, honey." Candy, hungry for a mother's touch, leaned into Audrey's hand, and even reached with her other hand to hold it to her face. Audrey's eyes glistened.

Laura told Audrey she'd placed her baby but didn't want to return to Morgantown. The girls confirmed her mother's mean behavior in the hospital. "I can go to the community college; I'd like to stay here, but I can't afford an apartment on my own. Sam, my boyfriend, was great, but I don't want to go to WVU, and he has a scholarship there. We're slipping apart. Good thing I found a good home for my baby, huh?"

A hush fell over the table. Michelle whispered that she didn't even have a boyfriend. The guy she thought she loved dropped her when he found out she was pregnant, and her father pushed her to abort. "We're Catholic, but he was ashamed and didn't want anyone to know I was pregnant. I wouldn't have an abortion, of course, so he sent me away as fast as he could."

Candy, Missy, and Cathy remained silent about their stories, except to agree their babies deserved life, and Audrey wondered. Cathy's baby was her grandson, after all.

Cathy dreaded being alone with her mother; where would they start? But Audrey thanked Cathy for letting her come, and Cathy told her mother she'd been forgiven by God; she couldn't withhold forgiveness.

"I have a lot of explaining to do, but I never wanted to send you away to school. Your father felt our life was too demanding to be 'bothered' with a child."

"Did you ever love him?"

"I thought I did. I was very poor as a child. My mother dragged me from cheap apartments to trailers and back again, following whichever man would provide her drugs and whiskey. Somehow, I managed to do well in school. After graduation, I got a job in Evan's club as a hostess. He is good-looking, and I was flattered by his attentions. He started taking me to his events and said I 'looked well' on his arm. He bought me beautiful clothes and jewelry, and took me to his house. I was overwhelmed. He finally told me I could be 'useful' to him and carefully trained me. Did you ever read *Pygmalion*?"

"In school. You were his creation, then?"

"I tried to be. I was desperate to please him. I guess I was like my mother."

"You were never addicted to whiskey or drugs."

"Sometimes I felt like drinking to oblivion. But I did learn something, living with her. Your father provided me with sleeping pills and Valium, but I only pretended to take them. When we conceived again and he discovered it wasn't a boy, he made me have an abortion. He even watched me take the Valium, so I put them under my tongue and swallowed to fool him. I began to hate him then."

"Why did you stay?"

"Where could I go? I was caught in his trap. When you ran away, I was suicidal. We searched and searched, hired private detectives, until he finally said—"

"I wasn't worth it."

"According to your father, you were ungrateful. You had a wealthy life afforded to you and you turned your back on it—but I thought you were brave and wonderful. He was *so* angry. He put me out of the house when the Mission approached us about granting custody, and said I wanted to see you."

"I was mean, Mom. I refused." Tears welled up in Cathy's eyes. "I'm sorry."

"I'm sorrier. You had a miserable life because I chose to please him. I understand. You must have felt alone and angry."

"I wish...I wish you'd told me. Just once, told me you loved me."

"I did," Audrey replied.

"Yeah, every time you left me at school."

"Oh, baby," Audrey cried.

"We'll go on from here, I guess. We can try, right?"

"Can I ask you what you did? How you survived all those months?"

Cathy looked down, then reached to switch off the bedside lamp. "Can we save that for later, when I know you better?"

"Do you...Do you know who the father of your baby is?"

"Yeah, I know." Cathy rolled over and faced the wall.

Cathy's tears rolled through her hair, soaking into the pillow. She wondered if her mother wept silently as well, trying to imagine her fifteen-year-old daughter, alone in a city she didn't know. *I was a prostitute; what will mother say to that?* She shuddered.

John came in early the next day and extricated the story of their relationship in his usual gentle way. Cathy expressed her bitterness about being abandoned in boarding schools, left out of vacations, and lonely when staying in empty dorms while all the other girls went away with their families. Audrey wept, confessing her fear of displeasing her husband and her total dependence on his pleasure. She lived in a palatial home, wore expensive clothes and jewelry, and entertained his wealthy clients—but he never loved her.

"He never wanted to be bothered with a child; he was angry she was a girl, and refused to have another. As soon as she was old enough, he sent her away." Audrey accepted the tissue John handed her and blotted her mottled face. "When we brought her home from the last school, he realized she'd grown up—become beautiful—and he thought she would be..."

"*Useful*, Mother. That's what he said. He took me to a reception, telling me to flirt with an older man, to act interested. He even made me put my hand on his thigh. Gross." *But excellent training for my profession.* "He wanted me to 'entertain' his business associates."

"But when Cathy ran away, you stood up to him? Perhaps for the first time?" John suggested.

"I saw her staring at me that night, watching me, and I knew she felt used—just like I did. I was never a friend, lover, or partner for Evan. I was a possession, a tool. She ran away, and I thought *good for her*! I admired her bravery. Evan was furious, ranting about all he had done for her. The schools, the clothes...She threw away wealth and position, he said, and when the Mission contacted us about placing her here and granting custody, he refused to let me go see her. When I insisted, he handed me divorce papers, told me I was no better than she was, and to get out."

Cathy fidgeted with her hands. In the quiet, she felt John's eyes on her. He had a way of doing that: saying nothing, waiting. Breaking the silence, she asked, "What are you going to do now, Mom?"

Audrey played with her hands, too. The two women shared a striking beauty: blonde hair, hazel eyes, and delicate bone structure. Evan thought they were perfect consorts for a man as long as they obeyed his wishes, never disagreeing with him.

"I have nothing but contempt and fury for men who use and discard women," John said. "Women deserve better. They should be protected and cherished, little girls especially."

Audrey looked up. "I'll land on my feet. Get a job as a hostess. I have experience, but it's been a while."

John smiled then. "I have some good news. Beth spoke to an attorney in Boston. He thinks the prenup can be broken and your husband can be compelled to at least recompense you for your years as a faithful companion—and certainly obtain child support for Cathy until she's eighteen. I assume the pittance of a settlement he gave you is about gone?"

"I have enough left to move to Columbus and pay a down payment and a few months' rent on a furnished apartment, but I haven't talked to Cathy about it. I'd like...I wish she'd let me help her with the baby. She'll have a hard time as a single mother." Her glance slid sideways, searching for her daughter's reaction.

Cathy was furious. She crossed her arms and kicked her foot. Her mother had been reduced to poverty!

"Can't you sell your jewelry?" Cathy asked.

With a sad smile, Audrey responded, "Your father said all those belonged to him—and I saw a photo of his new wife wearing the sapphire pendant and earrings."

"I haven't seen pictures, but I read she was in her twenties."

Audrey held out her hand, revealing her bare fingers. "He even took my wedding ring."

John intervened. "Let's hope the attorney can close some loopholes and secure support—at least enough to get you training for better employment." Looking back and forth between the two of them, he asked if they'd had enough for today.

Cathy took a deep breath. "I need to ask my mother one more thing."

"All right with you, Audrey?"

"Fair enough. I'm sure she has tons of questions."

Cathy's words stuck in her throat. She looked at John, who said nothing. He only tilted his head quizzically. Heaving a great sigh, the teenager looked at her mom, then looked away. She cleared her throat. Seeing her struggle, John patted her hand and waited. Tears glittered in her eyelashes.

"I wanted to know...I mean, I *did* watch you that night. You remember what I asked Father that morning, about should I sleep with him? And what he said? Did you ever...Did you have to do that—sleep with them—to entertain his associates?"

Audrey gasped and gripped her hands together until her knuckles were white.

Cathy sought John's eyes and saw only compassion in the look he gave them both.

"I...Uh..." Audrey stammered. She looked at Cathy and hung her head. "Not too often. Only when your father insisted." She laughed bitterly. "He always rewarded me with a striking piece of jewelry—which, of course, he kept."

Cathy bolted out of her chair. "God, I hate him!" She looked at John imploringly. "I need to find Missy."

John gave her the sweetest smile and nodded. "I'll see you Thursday—or earlier, if you want. Are you all right?"

"Yeah," she mumbled, pushing open the door and fleeing the small counseling office.

Cathy threw herself into Missy's arms and allowed her friend to guide her up the stairs to their room. *Missy seems to have a supernatural ability to sense these things*, Cathy thought. Of course she did; she and God were tight. Cathy found her in the living room, quietly reading her Bible, as if she waited for Cathy. She stood and opened her arms. Cathy sobbed, crying, "I hate him," over and over. Missy kept handing her tissues and holding her. Finally, her tears subsided, and she shared what she had learned her father had done to her mother: used her, degraded her, and threw her out with no support.

Missy didn't answer. Cathy thought, *what is it with these mature Christians? How can they remain silent? It's as if they wait for answers.* Which was exactly what Missy was doing, she realized. She soothed Cathy's tear-wet hair back from her eyes, and Cathy felt healing in the touch.

"I love you, Missy."

"I love you, too, girlie-girl." She sat back, still holding on to Cathy's arms. "God made a way for you."

"What do you mean?"

"Your mom survived the only way she knew how, and so did you. She'll understand, Cath. You can tell her about Wheeling and Donnie."

"Last night, she asked me how I'd survived and I was too ashamed to tell her. I asked her to wait."

"She must feel guilt, too. You can tell her about God's forgiveness."

"You're right!"

"Comfort her with the comfort God has given you. Then we'll begin the hard work of forgiving our fathers. Only God knows what made them the way they are."

"Missy, I hate him so much. God help me."

"He will."

"I left Mom in there with John."

"Good place."

"I have to go to her."

* * *

Audrey stayed in the little office with John after Cathy left, going through tissue after tissue. She told John her daughter must hate her. "I'm a common prostitute, John. What must she think of me?"

"She'll forgive you, Audrey."

"I wanted to lie, but I couldn't. She *knew*. How can she ever forgive me? She must never want to see me again. I shouldn't have come. I'll go pack and leave her alone."

"I wouldn't do that. She's more mature than you'd think, for her age. She's seen a lot in her young years. She'll forgive you."

"Do you really think so?"

"I know so. We are all sinners, saved by the grace of God. Jesus came to make all things new. Cathy found His grace and experienced His forgiveness. She won't withhold it from you."

"Why did she want Missy?"

"Missy is a good friend of Cathy's, and she's been a Christian all her life. She has overcome some horrible experiences by the grace of God. I'm sure Cathy's struggling with these revelations—more about your husband than you. She knows it's wrong to hate, and she's facing the depth of her hatred for him right now."

"She's not the only one. Aren't we supposed to hate evil?"

"We hate the sin—what he did to you, and to Cathy, was terribly wrong. Yes, it was evil, but Christ died for him too. We love the sinner and hate the sin."

"Pretty hard to do."

"Yes, it is. Impossible without God. Do you know God, Audrey?"

"Not as well as I need to, I guess."

"You'll be here for church services tomorrow?"

Audrey sighed. "She asked me to go to church with her. If Cathy wants me to stay, I will. I don't have anything else to do except go to the tiny little apartment in Belpre. I want to move here. I'd love to help her with the baby. She wants to keep the baby. Maybe if this lawyer gets anything for me, I can rent a place big enough for all of us."

"She'll be here at Hope House through her delivery and time enough after to get on her feet. We'll look at your options in the weeks to come. Let's pray the lawyer has some good answers for you." John reached into his inner coat pocket. "Here's his number. He has some questions for you, and he said you ought to call him today."

"On Saturday?"

"Beth said he sounded angry and ready to go to bat for you."

"I hope so; I need to have someone in my corner."

"You have a lot of someones in your corner: Beth, me, and the most powerful one of all: God Almighty, Lord of heaven and earth."

"I don't know how to thank you people."

"I forgot another someone: Cathy. Cathy's in your corner." When Audrey looked skeptical, John touched her hand. "Trust me on this. You haven't heard it all yet. Be patient." He stood. John was not a tall man, but his warm eyes behind thick lens washed over her in a powerful blessing.

Her Child Shall Lead Her

The next weekend, Audrey returned and noticed the changes in Cathy's body. Placing her hand on her daughter's belly, she said. "He's dropped. It won't be long now, Sweetie. Should I stay until he comes?"

Cathy dropped her head. "Go ahead with the move. Um...Missy and Miss Ginny will be with me. I'll be fine."

Audrey's disappointment showed on her face, but she smothered it with a brave smile. She didn't want to upset their tenuous relationship. She blinked back tears, and as soon as she put her suitcase in the room they would share, she sought out Beth.

"Good afternoon, Audrey, I stayed late to visit with you and Cathy. What's the report from the attorney?"

"It seems to be positive. The attorneys are negotiating. I changed my phone number because Evan called and threatened me, and my attorney recommended it. He said to let the attorneys work it out. But I wanted to talk to you about the birth. Cathy doesn't want me to stay for it. She told me to go ahead and move, but..." tears spilled out, "she wants Missy and Ginny with her. I know I haven't been much of a mother, but..."

Beth came around her desk and sat in the chair beside Audrey. "It's hard to explain how these girls become close. They walk the same paths and go through similar experiences. They laugh and cry together. They go to group therapy for months and face decisions about their babies. Missy's an unusual gal. She has strong faith. All the girls cling to her, and she was with Laura when she delivered. That said, you'll have a lifetime with your grandson, and you've made great strides in your relationship with Cathy."

"You think so?"

Beth squeezed her hand. "Yes, and we have more territory to travel this weekend. Are you ready?"

"I guess. This is hard, Beth."

"Life isn't easy. It has been a rough road for both of you this past year. Cathy is afraid."

"She's not the only one. Did John tell you what I told her?"

"She did."

"Do you think she can forgive me?"

"Without a doubt, Audrey."

"That's what John said. How can the two of you be so sure? I feel like a tramp. What daughter wants a mother like that?"

Cathy pushed open the door. Looking up, Beth moved out of the chair, allowing the teen to sit and take her mother's hand.

"One who's been there and done that too, Mom." Audrey stared. "It's how I survived. I was a prostitute."

"Oh, my baby. My poor baby!"

"Can you forgive me? I'm not exactly a daughter to be proud to have. I hate myself."

Audrey took her daughter in her arms. "You are my daughter. You survived. You didn't kill your baby. I killed your sister."

Cathy pulled back. "You had an abortion?" Audrey nodded in misery. "I get it," Cathy said. "Father didn't want another girl, right? Not a son, so get rid of it."

Audrey sobbed, and Cathy comforted her. Sniffing, her mother accepted her daughter's ministering embrace. "That's when I truly began to hate him."

Cathy let out a deep breath. "We'll have to work on that, Mom. Hating isn't good for either of us, but honestly, right now I could take a gun and shoot him—for both of us." The baby kicked, and since their bodies were pressed together, Audrey felt it.

She let out a broken laugh. "He'll miss his grandson, but I won't. My reward is great."

"I'm glad you can accept a prostitute's child."

"Solomon did. And God is the Author of life. I don't know Him well, but I know that."

A look of wonder crossed Cathy's face, and she turned to Beth. "Mom gave me a word from God. I wondered where He was that night. Now I know; He was right there. He's the Author of Life." She caressed her bulging belly. "He gave me this baby. I need to share this with Missy. She was raped, too," Cathy explained to her mother.

"May I fill in the details, Cathy?" Beth related Cathy's injuries from the brutal assault: the ruptured spleen, the bruised kidney, and the vagina so brutally torn it had to be repaired.

Audrey rocked her daughter in her arms, murmuring soothing words. For the first time, they shared a moment common to most mothers and daughters, and they basked in it.

Beth blinked back tears, watching them. "I'll leave you two a while," she said, slipping behind them, patting Cathy's shoulder on her way out.

* * *

She caught Ginny in the kitchen, preparing lunch. "You weren't in there long," the housemother said.

"Sometimes God moves in to heal, and I get out of the way."

"I know what you mean. He's the only one who can give the kind of healing these girls need, and I am awed every time."

Beth leaned against the doorframe.

Ginny stopped, blinking back tears. "I wish Myra had experienced it."

"Aw, Ginny, you showed her God's love. Someday she'll reach back for it."

Ginny took a deep breath. "I feel like I failed."

Beth took her by the arms and looked in her eyes. "You loved her. She wasn't ready."

Ginny shook the sad memories away. "Cathy told me she wanted Missy and me with her, and she knew it would hurt her mother's feelings."

"It did, but I was able to explain the relationships that form after months of sharing experiences, group therapy, laughter, and tears."

"This has been an unusually close group. Missy said the other night she thought they'd be friends forever."

"Missy has been the axis they've all revolved around. She's been a blessing in my life. She loves her baby, has never once rejected her, and the decision to place her was because she felt it was the best thing for the baby."

"I don't have favorites, but I do love that girl. She's special."

"She is."

"She's going to hurt big time when she surrenders the baby."

"She will, but she knows what she's doing and she hasn't wavered. I'm amazed at her ability to choose with such certainty and support Candy and Cathy's decisions."

"Joe's coming to dinner this evening."

Beth smiled. "Now there's a good kid, too. I knew he was a Christian the afternoon I took him home. Did you know he's asked Candy to marry him?"

"She's young. He's what...five, six years older?"

"Six, but John and pastor have both counseled with them. Joe's experience with his mom has given him a unique understanding of what Candy's been through. They're both older than their years."

Ginny wiped her hands on her apron. "Like so many of the girl-mothers who come here."

Beth stepped all the way into the kitchen. "Can I pour some lemonade? I have a feeling those two will need to replace some liquid soon."

"Do you want a sandwich, too?"

"I'll stick around until I'm sure they don't need me anymore." She returned to their earlier discussion. "Joe's determined to marry Candy before the baby comes so his name can be on the birth certificate."

"Candy wants to wait so she won't be big and pregnant."

Beth grinned. "We'll see."

"See what, Beth?" Cathy asked as she and her mother entered the room. Automatically, she laid out the silverware and napkins on the table, telling her mother to sit.

"You know about Joe and Candy, right?"

"Like, what else is anybody talking about around here?" Cathy giggled. Her mother watched, remembering what Beth told her about the girls laughing together.

"Can you believe Candy has snagged a boyfriend in her pregnant state, Mom? He wants to marry her now, and she wants to wait until after the baby comes. He's coming to dinner tonight. You'll get to meet him."

Audrey loved the sound of the word 'Mom' coming out of her daughter's mouth. "How interesting. Why does he want to marry before the birth if it's not his child?"

Beth explained his reasons, namely that Candy was keeping the baby and he wanted to be the father.

Audrey said she looked forward to meeting this young man. "I hope you find a good man to love you and your baby someday, Cathy—and Missy. I'm beginning to understand the relationships you girls share, especially you and Missy."

The conversation later revolved mostly around Candy and Joe, giving the mother and daughter a break from the intensity of the revelations they'd shared earlier. They giggled about the pregnant bride; laughter was as healing as tears. Audrey struggled, but soon caught her breath. "I haven't laughed much since my daughter was born. Now my daughter, who has suffered horribly, is teaching me to laugh."

The next day Cathy and Missy went with Audrey to look at apartments. Cathy told her that new mother Laura also needed a place to stay, and wondered if she could rent a three bedroom. Audrey didn't know Laura very well, but she remembered how close the girls were. However, she remained unsure about her finances. She explained to the landlord she was waiting on a divorce settlement, and he suggested that when she found out, they could adjust. She gave him a deposit on a two bedroom, and he gave her a key.

Since Joe and Candy had agreed the night before to go ahead with the wedding, Missy and Cathy eagerly discussed plans. They even stopped at a party supply store, where Audrey bought paper plates and napkins. Sunday morning after church, she pulled out to return to Belpre and pack up her few things: mostly clothes, along with some dishes and a few pots and pans.

Stanley

Waving at her mother's departing car, Cathy told Missy, "I didn't think she'd ever leave! I think it's time." Putting Missy's hand on her belly to feel it tighten, she added, "Isn't that a contraction?"

"I thought something was going on. She wanted to be here, though. Are you sure?"

"I'm sure. We're doing okay together, but, it's strange, getting to know your mother. She's been through a lot, and I went to the altar today and asked God's forgiveness for rejecting her. I realized I'd rejected her as much, or more, when I blamed her for rejecting me. We had all these years of distance, though, and I'd feel better with Ginny. I hope it works out, us living together."

"Miss Ginny says you'll stay here the full six weeks, and you guys can keep working on your relationship." Missy walked up the steps of Hope House, her arm around her friend. "You okay?"

"Yeah, but I feel like I wet my pants."

"If your water broke, you'd be standing in a puddle. Let's go see."

What they found was bloody show. While Cathy put on a pad, Missy brought her clean clothes and went to find Ginny. Michelle, Candy, and Laura gathered around Cathy. Laura, who'd recently given birth, was sympathetic and wanted assurance Missy would be with her at the hospital.

"Get her to sing to you, Cathy. That's how I made it through." She gave Missy a quick hug. "Thanks, Missy."

Missy shrugged. "It's how I get through everything. Singing to God."

Knowing her story, the girls appreciated what she told them. Missy was timing the contractions, and when they were steady at seven minutes, she went to find Ginny. The volunteer on call had already arrived, so Ginny and Missy loaded Cathy into the van and headed for the hospital. Ginny called Cathy's mother, who agreed to pack her household items and clothes and vacate her apartment in Belpre before returning to Columbus.

Missy did sing to Cathy, and she had a good delivery. She named her baby Stanley Robert, but no one knew why. She kept running her finger along his chin and smiling like she had an amazing secret that no one understood. Missy kissed her friend and little Stanley before she left the hospital at about midnight, needing to get some sleep before school.

Cathy returned to Hope House with her baby the next day. She had a bassinet set up in the room; after one night, she was eager for her mother to come help. Stanley was a good baby, but he was a new baby, and therefore wanted to eat every two hours. Audrey wept, seeing Cathy nurse the baby and his eager gulping. Evan had refused to allow her the joy and benefit of motherhood. He insisted on nannies for Cathy, and he was jealous of any attention she gave their child. When she was pregnant again, he cursed her for being careless. As soon as he found out it was another girl, he insisted on an abortion. Almost in retaliation, he sent Cathy off to boarding school.

Audrey was astounded when Cathy went downstairs three days after Stanley's birth; she remembered she had been made to stay in her bedroom for three weeks! When Stanley turned his head and his searching mouth nuzzled his mother's breast, the new grandmother fought tears and gently settled him on Cathy.

"You make me wish I could do this all over," she told her daughter.

"Let's find you a good man, Mom. You're not too old," Cathy teased.

"Maybe biologically, I'm technically young enough—I'm only 38. But I don't know if I'll ever be able to trust."

"Let's pray on it, Mom."

"What about you? Do you think you'll want to marry someday?"

Cathy shrugged. "Not now. Maybe someday."

The girls cooed over the baby and wanted to hold him, but Michelle and Missy agreed a baby needed more attention than they could give them at his point in their lives. They wanted to give their babies, if they ever had another, the time and energy they deserved. They were glad for Audrey and the developing relationship she and Cathy had.

Missy threw herself into wedding preparations. She went to school still, politely refusing a homebound teacher. Audrey took Candy out to shop for a dress, adding to the money Joe gave her, to buy a lovely cream empire-waist dress that fell to mid-calf. Cathy's mother helped Missy loop greenery and attach flowers down the bannister of the wide staircase. They bedecked an arch where the couple would stand. Beth and her husband, John and his wife, several church families, and all the Hope House girls joined the quiet celebration.

Audrey visited with Joe's mother, Martha, a tall reserved Appalachian woman who watched her son proudly as he calmly and seriously repeated his vows, looking at his pregnant bride with devotion. Audrey leaned and whispered, "I like your son. He's a fine man." Martha smiled.

After the cake and punch were served, the three Longs departed for their apartment. Everyone knew Joe intended to wait until after Candy had recovered from the birth before he took her on a honeymoon, which would be another hurdle for an abused young woman to face. Beth and John had both had their work cut out for them, preparing Candy for marriage. Joe Long did too; he vowed to give her all the time and tenderness she needed. He was indeed a special young man, and his mother showered Candy with love, a large factor in her healing.

Missy collapsed after the Longs left, and no one let her lift a finger in the cleanup. Beth teased her, giving her permission to have her own baby now. Missy laughed, but allowed as how she was ready. She loved everyone at Hope House, but she missed her mother and brother, and her beloved mountains.

The good news of the week was from Audrey's attorney. The court had ordered Evan to pay a settlement, granting child support until Cathy was 18, money for Audrey to obtain an education so that she could earn an adequate living, and alimony until her training was complete. He was livid, but the court also forbade further contact with his ex-wife and his daughter unless they initiated it. Laura helped them move into the three-bedroom apartment, and Audrey went to the community college to learn about her possibilities. Laura's parents agreed with her decision to complete high school in Columbus and go to the community college. Audrey started a medical secretarial course soon after Cathy and the baby, and Laura, moved into the apartment.

Missy had her little girl, and Laura spent a lot of time with her after the surrender. All the old and new Hope House girls attended the Christmas concert, where Missy did a solo and brought the house down with her performance. Her departure left a hole in all their hearts, but life moved ahead.

A teacher came to the apartment to finish preparing Cathy for her GED test, which she passed with flying colors. Her mother began her courses in the spring semester, and Cathy stayed home with the baby until summer. Michelle had her little boy, clinging to the phone while Missy sang to her. She was calm about the surrender, weeping a few tears, but moving in with a Catholic family from her church whose children were grown and gone. She got a scholarship to the University of Ohio in pre-med, and Cathy planned to start community college in the summer.

The Trial

Cathy had Stanley settled in for his morning nap when the phone rang. For some reason, she hesitated before answering. A female voice identified herself as Amy Rutledge, a prosecuting attorney from Wheeling, and told her Charles Foster had been charged with two counts of attempted murder, sexual assault in the first degree, and possession with intent to distribute. Candy would be subpoenaed to testify in the trial.

"You are young, Ms. Walker, but you are vital to the case and we'd appreciate your cooperation."

Cathy blew out a long breath. "Vermin like him shouldn't be allowed on the streets. I'll do what I can," she promised. When the attorney discovered Cathy had a baby, she traveled to Columbus to spend some time in preparation with the young mother.

Candy liked Ms. Rutledge, soon calling her Amy. They spent hours discussing the case while the attorney wrote copious notes. Eventually, Amy brought her to Wheeling, putting her and the baby up in a hotel. Ginny's daughter took personal leave day to help babysit while the team of prosecuting attorneys prepared Cathy for trial. They broke several times for her to nurse the baby, and Cathy drew strength from tending to her little one. At the end of a grueling day, Amy reminded Cathy she'd be asked the same questions on the stand; she could consider this a rehearsal, a practice run. Then the attorneys prepped her for cross examination, hammering her with cruel and degrading questions. Amy Rutledge told her colleagues she'd never met a woman with more courage, and she was only a kid! The trial would begin soon, she told Cathy, but they'd spend several days selecting a jury.

Cathy called all the Hope House girls for prayer. Audrey sought a leave of absence from school to be with her daughter for the ordeal, and they stayed in the hotel near the courthouse. The day of her testimony, Cathy was called to the stand; she raised her right hand and solemnly swore to tell the truth, the whole truth, and nothing but the truth, so help her God. She took a deep breath, avoided looking at Charles Foster and his attorneys, and scanned the crowd. Her eyes lit up when she saw John and Beth. John gave her a thumbs-up.

The prosecution made their case: she identified Charles, told how he had stormed into the hotel room and pushed his father, knocking him unconscious. She described the brutal and repeated rapes, the beatings that left her critically injured, and her hospitalization and recovery. She had begged Amy to conceal Stanley's birth because she didn't want Charles to even know about the baby. Several women in the jury blotted their eyes, and the defense went for blood to undo the damage she'd done.

"Ms. Walker," one of them began, "can you tell the Court why you were in a hotel with Charles Foster's father?"

"We were friends. He visited me sometimes."

"Friends? You were 'friends?' Ms. Walker, you are under oath. You were hired to be his 'friend,' weren't you? Isn't that the truth? Isn't it true that you were, in fact, a prostitute, a professional call girl working for Donnie Columbo from August 1991 through January of 1992?"

"We were friends."

"Answer the question, Ms. Walker. Were you a prostitute?"

Cathy lifted her chin. "Yes, but..."

"Thank you. And did you have other 'friends' during that time? Sometimes four or five nights out of the week?"

"Yes."

"Were you paid to engage in sexual activities with these men?"

Cathy shifted in her seat. The attorney waited, looking at the jury.

"Yes, Sir."

"Yes, Sir, what?"

"Yes, Sir, I was paid to have sex with men." Tears dripped down her chin. The judge handed her a box of tissues.

"But I wasn't paid to have sex with *him*." Candy pointed to Charles. "He raped me!"

"Objection, your honor."

"Strike that," the judge ordered.

The prosecution stood. "Your honor."

"You may proceed, Counselor."

Amy stood quietly in front of Cathy, who blew her nose into the tissues and grabbed another handful. She happened to look up and saw Beth weeping into her own tissues.

"Take your time, Cathy," Amy said, reminding her she was there. Cathy looked at her gratefully. "Ready?"

Cathy nodded. "How old were you when you began working for Donnie Caruso?"

"Fifteen." One woman on the jury gasped.

"Can you tell me why you began to work for him?"

"Objection. Irrelevant!"

Amy squared her shoulders and addressed the judge. "Defense counsel brought up the allegation of prostitution, Your Honor."

"Objection overruled. Please continue, Ms. Rutledge."

"Go ahead, Cathy. What were your circumstances when you began to work for Mr. Caruso?"

Cathy took a deep breath. "I was a runaway. I'd been living on the streets for several months. I was cold and hungry, and he offered me a job, no questions asked."

"Why did you run away from home? Were you abused?"

"Objection. Leading the witness. She can't testify, Your Honor."

"Sustained. Please restate, Ms. Rutledge."

"Why did you run away from home?"

"My father wanted me to 'entertain' his business associates. He told me to flirt with them, 'look at them adoringly,' 'be interested' in what they said. He made me put my hand on this old guy's thigh."

"Your father asked you to do that?"

61

"Yes, Ma'am."

"And you didn't like to do that?"

"It was *gross*."

One of the men on the jury chuckled, and the women looked appalled.

"So, you ran away."

"Yes, Ma'am."

"What was it like on the streets for a fifteen-year-old girl?"

"Objection, Your Honor."

"Get to the point, Ms. Rutledge."

Amy didn't ask anything, she just looked at Cathy.

"Donnie had a lady—she was a housemother, she said. She bought me something to eat and invited me to check out a job. At first, I just accompanied men to events—receptions, entertainments, that kind of stuff. After I'd been there a while, Donnie told me...there was more to the job. I was a virgin the first time," she blurted.

Amy hadn't known that, and her face showed her heartbreak for the girl.

The defense counsel appeared slightly shaken by the testimony, but undaunted, he stepped in front of the witness.

"Are you telling us the truth, Ms. Walker? You were in fact in the hotel room with Mr. Foster because you were a paid 'escort.' Isn't that the truth?"

"I may have been a child prostitute, but I've never been a liar."

"One last question. Who is Shirley Cooper?" the defense attorney asked.

"It's me," Cathy replied in a small voice.

"You? A fake name? In fact, you had a fake identity, didn't you? A fake ID? Shirley Cooper, age twenty-one?"

"Yes, Sir." Cathy hung her head

"Is that the truth?" The attorney for the defense strode back to the table, adding, "No further questions, Your Honor."

"You may step down, Ms. Walker," the judge said kindly. Then he recognized the prosecution attorney, who had raised her hand.

"Further questions, Ms. Rutledge?"

"Only a couple, Your Honor."

"Ms. Walker, why did you ask Donnie Caruso for a false ID?"

"I didn't want my parents to find me. I was saving for college, and I needed a Social Security number."

"How old are you now, Cathy?"

"Sixteen."

"Have you completed high school?"

"I got a GED. I'm enrolled in community college for the summer semester. I have a three-point-five grade point average."

Amy looked at the jury. "No further questions."

The prosecution called the doctor who had admitted Cathy to the hospital and the surgeon who took out her spleen, who also testified Cathy's vagina was torn from the violence she'd experienced and required internal stitches. Amy didn't call the doctor in Columbus who found the bruised kidney, to avoid having an obstetrician on the stand and keep private the revelations Cathy wanted to protect. She had enough to nail the guy, and they hadn't even started with the drugs.

Cathy was called back to the stand to testify about the assault on Mr. Foster. She described how Charles had pushed him, and he was knocked unconscious on the leg of the chair. "When his son finally passed out, I managed to crawl over to his father. I untied him and bathed his face. He called for help."

"And then what happened?" Amy Rutledge asked.

"The police arrived and asked me if Stan did that to me. I said no, and pointed to the bedroom. I must have passed out then. I don't remember the trip to the hospital."

The defense counsel stood. "She was able to crawl across the room and bathe his face. Are we seriously going to accept the testimony of a prostitute? My client is a respected businessman—"

"He beat his own father! He told me I'd never get his father's money. He wanted it all for himself!" The courtroom went into an uproar, defense objecting and demanding Cathy's remarks be stricken. Several women in the jury were crying out while Cathy wept.

The judge pounded his gavel demanding order, but he spoke gently to Cathy, dismissing her. Then he declared the court recessed for the day.

Cathy walked toward the prosecuting attorneys' desk.

Charles stood and spat, screaming names at her. The bailiff stepped between him and the girl, and Amy put her arm around her to shield her while his attorneys told him to shut up.

Beth and John pushed forward, introducing themselves. Cathy fell into their arms, and Amy was relieved her witness had moral support. "She did a wonderful job." Amy patted her shoulder. "One of the best witnesses I've ever had." She told them where she was staying, and they agreed to take her to the hotel.

"I need Stanley. I'm dripping all over myself. I hope that..." Cathy fought the urge to swear, "*asterisk* didn't curdle my milk!"

They couldn't help it. John, Beth, and Amy had to laugh.

"Get her a beer," Amy said. "I hear that's good for mother's milk."

"I wonder where Stan is. Why isn't he here?"

A gentleman approached them as they moved into a side hallway. "Ms. Walker, I'm Allen Overstreet, attorney to Stan Foster." He gave her his card. "I've been looking for Shirley Cooper, and when I found out about the trial, I knew I'd find you here. I also have his power of attorney." He showed Cathy some documents. "I know this was a terrible experience for you, but I must talk to you. Stan sent me."

"Where is he?" Cathy asked. "Is he okay?"

"I regret to tell you, he's critically ill."

Cathy sank onto a wooden bench. "I'm so sorry. Can you tell him...Tell him Cathy Walker loves him."

"I must speak with you, and perhaps we have time for you to tell him that yourself, if you'd like."

"Tell him he's the grandfather of a beautiful baby boy. I named him Stanley Robert Walker."

"Why Robert?"

"I saw his signature many times. He always signed Stanley R. Foster. Robert was the most common R name I thought of, so..."

Allen chuckled. "It's Raymond, but Stan will love it. I'll tell him." He looked at Beth and John. "Are you taking her?" They said they were. He asked if he could come by in the morning.

"If I don't have to come back here," she said.

Allen Overstreet chuckled. "I don't think the prosecution needs any more testimony, and I'm sure the defense doesn't want to see you within a hundred miles of this courtroom. You did an excellent job!"

"Will he get better? Stan?"

"No. He's hanging by a thread, hoping to get news of you. I'll call him tonight and tell him about little Stanley. You're an amazing young lady."

"You do what you have to do; live one day at a time, as God gives you strength."

"No wonder Stan loves you so much, Cathy." Allen touched her cheek briefly and told her he'd see her the next morning at about nine, and be off to Chicago. "Maybe I can take some pictures of the baby."

"He has his grandfather's chin and his blue, blue eyes."

Allen blinked, took her hand and kissed it, then bade them good night.

Beth put her arm around the teen and guided her out a side door. On the way to the hotel, she and John expressed admiration for her good job on the stand.

"I'm sure justice will be served because of your courage," John told her. He put his arm around Cathy's shoulders and pulled her close. "Well, Miss Cathy, do you have any more surprises for us?"

"No, I think that's got it. He's a wonderful old man. He didn't ask for sex much. Mostly we just talked and cuddled."

"And that's why you named the baby Stanley," Beth said. "I wondered."

"I named him for the first man who ever loved me," Cathy said.

Beth stopped walking and pulled Cathy into her arms. "He's right. You are a remarkable young woman, and I'm proud to know you."

"My bloused is soaked, Beth. Can we just go?"

Once again, they laughed. They took her to the hotel, and Stanley was eager to see his mother. Audrey told Cathy he'd taken the bottles she'd left for him, but he wasn't happy about it.

"What a day!" John said. "Are you ready to drive back to Columbus?"

"I hated to leave my kids this long, but I wouldn't have missed this for anything!" Beth gave Cathy and hug, and they left.

The Old Man

Cathy left for Chicago with Allen before the verdict was returned. Amy called later to tell Cathy he was found guilty on all counts. The prosecution introduced as further evidence a will obtained from Charles Foster's briefcase, leaving all his father's holdings to his son, awaiting his signature.

As much as Cathy wanted to hear the guilty verdict, she wanted to get to Stan before he died. Allen forwarded her a ticket and met her at the airport. He took her bag, and she shuffled the sleeping baby to her shoulder. They drove straight to the house. When Allen called Stan was sleeping, but the nurse said he brightened considerably when she showed him the pictures of Stanley.

The elderly butler who opened the door regarded her with cool disdain, but led the way to the bedroom, tapping softly on the door. A middle-aged woman in a nurse's uniform answered the door. "Come in, Dear. Mr. Foster is waiting." She turned to the butler. "Thank you, Clyde. Come in, Mr. Overstreet."

Cathy hesitated, taking in the medical equipment, IVs and oxygen, but when she looked at the frail figure on the bed, she shoved Stanley in the nurse's arms and rushed to Stan's side.

"I'm glad you came. I'm sorry, Cathy—it is Cathy, right?"

"Cathy Walker. I'm sorry I deceived you, Stan."

"You're apologizing to me? You were fifteen years old! I had no right. It was unforgiveable what I did to you, child."

Cathy brushed her lips on his sunken cheek, and he reached for her hand. "Allen told me what you said, about naming the baby."

Cathy smiled at him. "I named him after the first man who ever loved me."

A lone tear trickled down the weathered cheek. "May I see him?"

She brightened and took him out of the nurse's arms, bringing him to the bedside. Leaning down, she pushed back the blanket, and Stanley opened his bright blue eyes. "He looks like his grandfather, doesn't he?" She ran her finger under his square jaw. "See, he has your chin and your eyes. He's a good baby."

Stan struggled to sit higher, and the nurse and Allen Overstreet helped him, leaning him against the pillows they banked behind him.

Cathy gently set the baby in his arms, and he gazed at his grandson in wonder.

"How did you do this?" he asked.

She giggled. "The way every woman in the world does, Stan. It was a lot of work, but isn't he worth it?"

"Where did you live? I looked and looked for you."

Seeing him tire before her eyes, Cathy gathered the baby up. "I lived in a maternity home in Columbus, Ohio." Stanley began to fuss. "He's hungry. May I feed him?"

Allen pushed a chair beside the bed, and Cathy nursed him. Stan watched, fascinated. He looked at the lush fullness of her breast, remembering the pert little peaks he once knew intimately. She looked up and caught him. He flushed.

"He looks healthy."

"He is—he's in the seventieth percentile."

"I'm happy you brought him."

The nurse, Mrs. Browning, suggested they allow the patient to rest. Perhaps Cathy could visit again later.

Cathy leaned over the bed and kissed him. "I do love you, Stan. You were always good to me. Always."

He shook his head, but his eyes fluttered.

Cathy followed Allen out of the room.

"They have a bedroom prepared for you." Allen looked around the hall.

Mrs. Browning closed the door softly and opened the door to the room immediately to the right of Stan's room. "I told Clyde to put your things in here."

The lawyer followed her into the bedroom, noticing she wasn't overwhelmed in the beautiful old mansion, and he commented upon it.

"I lived in a house like this in Boston, whenever my father allowed me to come home from school," she said.

"Do you mind? I have some papers for you to sign, and some things to go over with you."

"I have to give Stanley the other breast, but I have a cover. I didn't bother in there because I didn't want him to get cranked up. He can get a little loud and demanding when he's hungry."

"I have two sons, ages twelve and fourteen, but I remember when they were babies. If you want me to step out..."

Stanley was busy nuzzling her breast, hungrily smelling the rest of his meal. They both laughed, and Cathy told the lawyer if he didn't mind, he could stay.

"Stan was happier and brighter than I've seen him in months, Cathy. Thank you for coming and bringing the baby."

"I do love him. I guess that's hard for you to understand, given the circumstances, but he was kind to me. He didn't ask for much; we mostly cuddled. He liked to sleep beside me."

"When he found you how young you were, he was horrified and cursed Donnie for doing that to you."

"What's done is done."

"Why didn't you have an abortion?"

Cathy paused. "When I was released from the hospital, I was send to a Christian homeless shelter. I went to chapel every day, and when I missed my period for two months, they took me to a Christian pregnancy center. I saw the fetal models and talked to the ladies there. Charlie...Charlie was an awful man, and what he did to me..." She shuddered. "But he was Stan's too, in a way, and I focused on that. I pretended he was Stan's baby. I knew he wasn't—we hadn't done that in a while. Had sex, I mean. Besides, Donnie insisted we use condoms every time, but of course Charlie didn't."

"You pretended he was Stan's?"

"I've always thought of him as Stan's. I worried about whether Charlie's genes would make the baby mental or something, but the counselor at Hope House assured me he would be the way he was taught. It was drugs that made Charlie violent like that."

"Charlie's mother spoiled him. I've known the family for years, and she made excuses for him all his life. Stan tried to make him face the consequences of his bad behavior, but she paid his way out of all his mistakes."

"He's evil."

"He is the meanest man I've ever met. He was cruel to his mother and father. I think you'll be a wonderful mother."

She gently took the baby off the breast and covered herself. "I'll try, with all my heart."

Allen reached into his briefcase. "Stan had me rewrite his will. The one I brought left you sufficient funds to attend any university you chose, but of course it named you as Shirley Cooper. And once he found out about Stanley, he still set aside those monies for you and put everything else in trust for the baby." Cathy's eyes rounded. "He wanted to change the baby's name to Foster, but he said if you didn't want to do that, because of Charlie, he'd go ahead anyway. He specifically said the name change would not be a condition."

Cathy piled pillows on the huge bed to form a cushion for Stanley and placed the baby in the hollow she created, too stunned to say anything.

"I'll get a crib in here for you. How long do you plan to stay?"

"How long does he have?"

"I thought he'd die a month ago, but he rallied for you—and Stanley."

"Thank God I got here in time."

"You made an old man very happy."

She smiled at the memory. "He told me that once."

Allen handed her the papers. "This is the name change form on top. Do you want to sign it?"

"I always thought of Stanley as Stan's baby. I'll sign."

"You are too young to be executor for the estate and the trust. We'll appoint someone from Stan's money management company until you're of age. How do you handle your rent and so on? Have you been emancipated?"

"Thank God, my mother and I have reconciled. My father divorced her, and she came to me. We worked through a lot of forgiveness with the help of the counselors from the home. We live together now. She's going to a medical secretarial program, and I'll start college this summer. We'll trade off taking care of the baby."

"That's good news, Cathy."

"Life's too short to be bitter."

"You are entirely too wise to be sixteen." Allen gathered up his papers and stood. "I'll get this filed. Stan suggested he write you a check because it will take a while to get all this settled."

"He doesn't owe me a thing, Mr. Overstreet."

"I beg to differ. You've given him a grandson—and a lot of devotion." He went to shake her hand, but instead brought it to his lips.

"Would you tell Mrs. Browning to wake me when Stan is awake? I'll lie down myself."

"We'll get a crib in here for you as soon as possible."

When the nurse tapped on her door, Cathy sat up, pushing her sleep-tangled hair off her face. Stanley stirred beside her. "Come in," she called.

"You got a little rest; good for you.

Does he still get you up at night?"

"Yes, Ma'am. He's not on a lot of solid foods yet. He mostly gets breast milk."

"Excellent! Mr. Foster is awake and asking for you."

Cathy changed the baby, who smiled happily but immediately began to nuzzle when she picked him up. "You little piglet, can you wait a minute?" She chuckled and hoisted him to her shoulder. "Let's go see Daddy," and she wished it was so.

Stan was looking at the door, waiting for it to open. When it opened and he saw Cathy framed in the light, he beamed and held out his hand. She moved to his side quickly and kissed his cheek.

"Thank you for coming."

"Thank you for looking for me."

"Did Allen ask you about the name? You don't have to do that. It won't change a thing."

"I pretended you were Stanley's daddy anyway. I wish you were. You wouldn't consider...you couldn't adopt him, could you?"

The old man's eyes brightened. "Bring me the phone and dial this number." He recited a number for her. When Allen Overstreet answered, Stan said, "Cathy's come up with a brilliant idea. She suggested I adopt the baby. Wouldn't that be the most direct thing to do? It would make him my direct heir." He listened. "I understand, but if we filed...Get on it then!" He handed the phone back to Cathy.

Allen was chuckling. "You are something else, young lady. This is the straightforward way to proceed, but we must move quickly. He hasn't got much time. You put me to work again! I'll draw this up and come back this evening with yet another set of papers to sign. Let me get this straight; you want Stan to adopt the baby, is that correct?"

"If he will, and only if he wants to."

"There's not a doubt. Okay, see you later."

Cathy hung the phone up and removed it from the bed. Stan reached for her hand, and she took his.

"Where's the baby?"

"He's on the floor. He's got a blanket with all kinds of toys on it. But he's getting hungry again. Do you mind?"

"I love to watch you."

She blushed, but picked Stanley up and settled him on her breast.

Stan watched her lean over the baby, her blonde curls dangling onto his cheek, her eyes filled with love and tenderness. He sighed.

"Are we tiring you?"

"No, no. You're a good mother, Cathy, and you're so young. How can you be such a good mother at your age?"

"I've lived too much. I pretended you were his father, and I love his father."

Stan tried to blink away tears, but they trickled on down his cheeks. "Allen will make it happen. Even if it's completed after—"

"Shh. You'll always be his daddy, Stan."

"I don't deserve your kindness, after what I did to you. Please forgive me."

"Do you believe in Jesus?"

"Of course I do!"

"Do you believe He died on the cross for our sins?"

"I do."

"And He rose again?"

"I didn't act like it, but I do. I'd been alone a long time. Even before she died, Rosemary and I hadn't lived together as man and wife for some time. We fought over our son. She indulged him, covered for him, and destroyed him. She had been dead for three years when Donnie saw me in the hotel bar, nursing a drink. He asked me if I was lonely and told me he could cure that. I had no idea how young you were!"

"I wish you'd be here to help me train him. I want him to be like you. You were kind and gentle. I'll always be grateful for that, and because you believe, I'll see you in heaven."

"God sent you to me."

Cathy burped the baby on her shoulder and laid him on his blanket, where he kicked and reached up for the toys overhead. She pulled the chair up closer to Stan's bedside and put her head on his chest. He sifted her soft hair through his fingers and closed his eyes. "I pray Allen can get this done in time."

Mrs. Browning came in quietly, watching the scene before her. She smiled at Cathy, who lifted tear-stained eyes. "Shh," the nurse whispered. "He's calm and peaceful, resting quietly." She exchanged the nearly empty IV for a full one. "You've been good for him, Miss Cathy." She looked down at the baby, stretched as far as he could to reach a toy on the blanket. "He's a good baby." Cathy nodded. "Do you want to come downstairs for dinner?"

"Could I eat in here, or would the smell of food make him nauseous?"

"I don't think so. I'll have Clyde bring in a tray table."

By the time Clyde arrived, the baby had fallen asleep. Cathy had lain her head beside Stan, her lips pressed on his hand. Feeling the butler's stare, she lifted her head.

"I'll set this here and bring your dinner in a few moments. Look, Mr. Foster's smiling."

"Shh, he's asleep."

"I'm not, My Angel."

Cathy laughed. "You must be the only man in the world who'd call a prostitute an angel."

Stan opened his eyes. "Jesus loved prostitutes and sinners. I guess that includes both of us." He brought her hand to his lips and kissed it.

Clyde took in the looks of love in both their eyes and realized he'd judged this girl too harshly. He cleared his throat. "Miss Cathy wants to eat in here, Sir."

"Fine. That's fine, Clyde. We don't have too much time."

"Yes, Sir. As you wish." He turned and bowed slightly. "I'll be back with your supper in a moment, Miss Cathy."

"Where's the baby?" Stan asked.

"Asleep in the floor. But you watch. When he smells food, he'll be demanding his own."

"What does he eat?"

"Mostly mommy milk for now. He's only five months old."

"He has a good mother. He'll be a fine man."

"Like his daddy. I'm so glad you'll be his daddy!"

The door pushed opened and Allen entered, with yet more papers in his hand. "All right you two, if you come up with any more work for me, I'll be up all night." He looked at Stan. "This visit has been good for you."

"You bet."

"Cathy, can you help me? We need to sit him up so he can sign. I also brought a check for you, made out to Cathy Walker."

"Thanks, Allen. You thought of everything." He signed the check. "And the adoption papers?"

"Right here. Sign on this line." The patient carefully wrote his name. "And you, Cathy, can you sign here?"

"You bet. This makes my dream come true."

Stanley lifted his head and made a noise.

"My goodness, I didn't know he was here," Allen said. "I put a pack and play in your room."

"Thanks. I was afraid I'd roll over on him this afternoon."

"I'm sorry I didn't think of that." Allen looked through the papers, checking for signatures. "Can you initial here, Sir?"

Stan dutifully scribbled his initials. "Are you sure we can do this?"

"We had several researchers checking every detail. We're good, Stan."

"This squares away the inheritance?"

"He's legally yours. I talked to Judge O'Conner and explained the circumstances. He'll sign in the morning."

"I'll wait."

The next morning, Stan was noticeably weaker, but still there. Allen called with the report that the deed was accomplished, and he'd sent the papers off to the Ohio bureau of vital records. Stan was the legal father of Stanley Raymond Foster, Jr.

He smiled and reached for Cathy's hand.

"I'll teach him to honor his father," she promised.

"He'll be a wealthy man, Cathy."

"You don't have to do that, Stan. You don't owe me anything."

"My precious angel. I love you." Stanley began complaining. "I believe our son—can I say that, our son? —is looking for his mommy."

Cathy picked him up from his blanket and laid him beside Stan, who let him cling to his finger while she changed him. She sat beside the bed to feed him, and she noticed Stan looking at her breast.

God forgive him, he wanted to caress her breast one last time, and she knew it.

When the baby was full, Cathy took him to her room and put him in the pack and play. Returning to Stan's room, she lay beside him. He opened his eyes.

"Can we lie together for old time's sake? Like we used to?" God forgive her, she unbuttoned her blouse and put his hand on her. He smiled and brushed his lips on her forehead and went to sleep, for the last time.

Mrs. Browning slipped in. She quietly removed Mr. Foster's hand. Cathy stirred. "He's gone, Sweetie," she said gently.

Cathy sat up, shoved her fist in her mouth, and wept. Mrs. Brown drew her to her bosom. "I loved him," Cathy said.

"I know you did. We all saw it. He never stopped talking about you from the moment Mr. Overstreet called. He loved you, my dear."

"He did. He was the first man who ever loved me in my whole life."

Two days later, on a quiet, windswept hill overlooking the city, Cathy stood beside Allen at the back of a large crowd. She'd left Stanley back at the house with Mrs. Browning. When her shoulders began to shake, she was surprised to feel someone put an arm around her and lean her into his strength. Looking up, she saw Clyde. His eyes glistened. "You arrived just in time, Miss Cathy. You made an old man very happy."

She'd heard it before.

The Odd Couple

When the trio, Allen, Clyde, and Cathy returned to the house, Allen stayed long enough to share a sandwich. Cathy would leave in the morning. The house would be sold and the money added to the estate. "I've ordered a car to take you to the airport tomorrow," Allen said.

"I'll take her, Mr. Overstreet," Clyde said. She'll need help with the baby."

"That would be better, Clyde. Thank you." Allen reached into his coat pocket and handed her an envelope. "Stan dictated this to me before I left for Wheeling, and the check is in there also."

"I'd rather have him to help me bring up his son."

"Miss Cathy, I must apologize," Clyde said. "We heard all kinds of things, and I believed the worst. I thought you were after Mr. Foster's money. I was wrong. I saw you with him, and the way he looked at you. I'm sorry."

"Clyde," she said, covering his hand with her own, "I understand. Our... relationship was unusual, to say the least." She turned to Allen, "Stan did take care of all the staff?"

"He did, Cathy. They are pensioned generously for life." He rose and kissed her cheek. "You take care now, and if you're ever this way, be sure to bring little Stanley by to see us. You have my card. We'll be in touch as all this works out."

"If you're ever down our way, let me know. I'd love to see you."

Audrey picked her up at the airport, hugging her and little Stanley. "I've missed you! How are you doing, honey?"

"I'm glad I went, Mom. You won't believe all that's happened. I'm sorry I didn't call more—he was almost gone when I got there. I almost missed him."

"We need to begin at the beginning. This man was the father of the man you testified against?"

"He was, but he was nothing like him!"

"I thought...wasn't he...didn't he...?"

"He hired me, Mom, but he didn't want much. We mostly cuddled."

"And you named the baby after him?"

"I did, and before he passed, he adopted Stanley. His name is now Stanley Randolph Foster, Jr. I guessed the 'R' was Robert, but it was Randolph."

Audrey stared at her, coming to a complete stop as they walked to the car.

"He is a wealthy man, Mom, and he left everything to his grandson—his legal son."

"Oh, my—tell me how this happened."

In the car on the way to the apartment, Cathy described her time in Chicago. When they arrived, Audrey played with the baby while Cathy retrieved the letter from her diaper bag.

"Dearest Shirley, I pray Allen finds you. I have upmost respect for you, my dear, and I want you to have sufficient funds to fulfill your dream of college. I want you to go to a fine school. You are a smart young woman, and you've been the best thing in my life. I appreciate you. I can almost believe you loved me, in a strange sort of way. We were an odd couple, Shirley. Thank you, from the depths of my heart. I've searched to find you and make sure you are well. I'm sorry beyond words for what Charles did to you. Be blessed, be happy. Love, Stan."

"How sweet," Audrey said.

"He was a sweet old man." Cathy had already determined no one would ever know Stan took her virginity at 15. "He knew me as Shirley Cooper, age 21. He was horrified to learn how young I was. I wish Allen hadn't told him." As she inserted the letter back into the envelope, the check fluttered out. Unfolding it, her jaw dropped. "This is a mistake."

"What?"

"This check. It's for $500,000.00. I have to call Allen."

But when she called Allen, he told her that was correct. Stan wanted her to go to any college she wanted: he said it was the least he could do.

"I can't believe this."

Allen chuckled. "I'll have to tell Clyde. Sleep well, Cathy, dream sweet dreams and big dreams, make the old man proud. I know you will. Keep in touch."

Cathy immediately began researching Christian colleges. She wanted a degree in Christian counseling, and finally narrowed it down to Wheaton College in Wheaton, Illinois. She had to create a GPA at the community college and transfer, if she could get in. Meanwhile, her mother could complete her medical secretarial course. Cathy didn't have to work, thanks to her benefactor, so she applied herself to her studies, finished two years with a 4.0, and applied for Wheaton.

Running into the apartment, waving a letter from the college, she screamed, "I got in!" They gave notice to the landlord, packed up the car, and left for Illinois. Wheaton was north of Chicago, and she called Allen first thing.

"I was excited to hear you were coming. I've spoken to Clyde, and my wife can hardly wait to meet you. Where are you?"

She told him the hotel where they were staying while they looked for an apartment. He suggested a house with a yard for Stanley, which she could afford since the trust sent a generous check for him every quarter. He told her how to get down to Chicago on the commuter train, and they planned a day the next week to come down for the night. In the meantime, she located a suitable small house, three bedrooms, with a yard, and they got settled.

When they got off the train, Clyde met them, taking her in his arms and planting a big kiss on her cheek. "Miss Cathy, it's good to see you." He turned to bow to Audrey.

Stanley tugged on his mother's hand. "Mama, who is this man?"

Cathy laughed and picked him up. "This is Mr. Clyde, baby. He's a friend of your daddy's."

The boy studied Clyde. "My daddy went to heaven."

"Yes, he did. He was a fine man, Stanley."

"How do you know my name?"

"It was your father's name, and I met you when you were a baby."

"Clyde, this is my mother, Audrey Walker."

"She is as beautiful as you are, Miss Cathy." He took her hand in both of his.

Stanley struggled out of his mother's arms, but she held him firmly by the hand as Clyde led them to the car, apologizing that Mr. Allen couldn't be there. He was delayed at the office. Clyde explained they'd go directly to his home for supper. He was prepared this time—he had a car seat for Stanley.

"Would it be out of the way to swing by Stan's house? I'd love to show it to Mother."

"It's quite near the Overstreet's home." Clyde slowed the car as they drove by; a couple of blocks later, he turned right and continued several blocks before coming to a stop. He walked them to the front door and Cecilia Overstreet welcomed them inside. Allen was in the shower, but he would be down soon.

"Miss Audrey, may I get you some refreshment?" Clyde asked, giving a courtly bow.

Cecilia laughed. "Clyde, you aren't a butler here. Let me do the honors. Sit."

The poor man looked as awkward as he must have felt, perching on the edge of the chair.

Audrey leaned forward and patted his arm. "Please, you mustn't call me 'Miss Audrey.' It makes me feel a hundred years old."

"Oh, no, you don't look old. You look too young to be Miss Cathy's mother!" He turned to Cathy. "We are happy to see you, and happier still you'll be nearby for a while."

"About three years, depending on how my credits transfer—and, Clyde, you must drop the 'Miss Cathy,' as well. Have you heard from Mrs. Browning?"

"Not in a while—last we heard, she still works for hospice."

At that point Allen came in, carrying a tray of drinks for his wife. Beaming, he pulled Cathy into a huge hug, lifting her off her feet.

"Who are you? Another friend of my daddy's?"

Allen ruffled Stanley's hair and squatted to be eye level. "I am, and don't you talk well for your age."

"Mama says I make her ears hurt."

Cathy chuckled. "He didn't talk for the longest time and now he doesn't stop!"

"My, he looks like Stan, doesn't he?"

"I think so," she agreed.

Allen called his boys down for dinner and introduced everyone. The teenagers were quite taken with the precocious little boy, and after dinner took him in the yard to see the Koi pond. Cathy told them her plans to complete her undergraduate degree in psychology and get a Master's in Clinical Mental Health Counseling. She would meet with a faculty member next week. They had arranged for the Walkers to stay in a nearby hotel, and when Stanley began to wear down, Clyde dropped them off, promising to show them Chicago the next day.

He picked them up in the morning and drove them down the shore of Lake Michigan, out to Millennium Park and to the Museum of Science and Industry. Stanley asked thousands of questions before he conked out on Clyde's shoulder. He took them back to the hotel and asked if they wanted to go to dinner that evening. Cathy was ready to call it a day. Audrey graciously accepted, but wanted time to refresh. Clyde agreed to pick her up in two hours.

"Mom, I think Clyde has a thing for you."

"Phooey," she snorted, but a blush crept up her cheeks, and she put on her newest dress.

Cathy had supper with Stanley in the room, and they watched a cartoon movie; Clyde and Audrey did the town. Cathy turned out the light at ten and heard her mother come in much later. They left the next day, after having lunch with Allen downtown, near his office, and Clyde promised to come and see them in Wheaton.

Classes started in late August. Audrey found a job in a medical office, and Stanley attended preschool. Clyde visited regularly and found a job managing the dining services at the college before he moved to Wheaton. His pension kept him comfortably, he explained, but he couldn't sit around doing nothing. He fixed dinner for them on his nights off.

In a year, Audrey and Clyde were married. Cathy managed the house by herself, and her mother moved to Clyde's apartment–Stanley was happy at both places.

Although she missed Columbus and planned to return one day, Cathy immersed herself in her studies. Between maintaining a high GPA and being a single mother, she hardly had a moment to spare. They went to Chicago to see the Overstreets occasionally, and on one of their trips, Cathy took Stanley to his father's grave. He asked questions about him, and Allen took him to see Foster House, a place where families with sick children could stay near the hospital, explaining his father donated the facility.

Her senior year, Cathy enrolled in a seminar class entitled 'The Theology of Helping.' The small group of honors students was led by a PhD candidate. David Taylor was bright, witty, and challenging–and particularly interested in one Cathy Walker, who appeared oblivious to his overtures. He was a good-looking man, classically tall, dark, and handsome. But unlike many of the girls in his classes, she seemed immune to his charms.

* * *

One crisp autumn day, he caught up with her after class. He asked if she'd like a cup of coffee, but she told him she couldn't. "You don't date, do you, Ms. Walker?"

"No, I'm too busy."

"What keeps you so busy?"

A young lad, about five, cried "Mama" and ran toward her, hurling himself in her arms. Laughing, she twirled him around.

"My son, Mr. Taylor. Stanley, this is Mama's teacher." She put him down, and he politely stuck out his hand.

"Good afternoon, Mr. Taylor. Would you like to come to our house?"

"I would, but you should ask your mother."

"Where's Nana, Stanley?"

He pointed to the nearby car, where Audrey was closing the door. "He saw you, and that was it, dear," the grandmother said.

"Mr. Taylor, it appears you'll meet my entire family this afternoon. My mother, Audrey Davenport."

His brown eyes twinkling, David took Audrey's hand. "Delighted. I assume everyone tells you your daughter looks just like you."

"Thank God," Cathy muttered.

"I was just going to meet my husband for a cup of coffee. Won't you join us?"

"Mom, Mr. Taylor is my teacher."

"I'd love to," he replied, avoiding Cathy's glance.

"Come on, Mr. Taylor." Stanley took his hand and tugged him along. David chuckled. Cathy sighed.

"Is it terribly bad, Ms. Walker?"

"It's lovely, but isn't it inappropriate?"

"Are you going to sue me for harassment?" he teased.

"Am I going to be accused of using inappropriate methods of obtaining my grade?"

"I've looked at your grades, and I don't think anyone would believe you didn't earn the grade you'll get from me." He stopped and crossed his heart. "But I promise I'll grade you fair and square and tell you no questions before the test."

"You may think this is funny, Mr. Taylor, but I take my academic career seriously. I plan to go for my Master's next year."

Stanley let go of David's hand when he saw Clyde, who picked him up. Cathy introduced him and together the group crowed into a booth in the student center.

"Mama, can I...may I have a cookie? We had an apple for snack."

"With milk, okay?" The boy happily agreed and crawled on Audrey's lap.

"Tomorrow's no school day, right?"

"Right." Cathy confirmed.

"And we're gonna rake leaves, right?"

"Right again."

"Wanna come rake leaves, Mr. Taylor? Mama says we can roast hot dogs after."

"I'm sure Mr. Taylor has plenty of better things to do than rake leaves, Stanley."

David's mouth quivered. "A day in the autumn sunshine would be fun, if it's all right with your mother." Cathy rolled her eyes, and David laughed then. "I happen to be a big fan of hot dogs. I'll bring the marshmallows, Hershey bars, and graham crackers."

"Are you always this incorrigible?" Cathy asked.

"My mom had five boys, and she says I'm the worst of the lot. I'm the baby." He turned to the boy. "Where do you live, Stanley?"

"506 Erie Avenue," the lad told him. "Be there by ten. Nine would be better."

"Stanley!"

David couldn't help it. He laughed, thinking he'd gladly be courted by her little boy, since no father appeared to be in the picture.

Thus began the unlikely courtship of David Taylor and Cathy Walker, who'd never had a real date in her life. Her grades in his class were hard-earned because he was ruthless with her, but he was an excellent teacher. David was drawn to this sensitive young woman, but she kept secrets, and she kept him at arm's length. She was evasive about Stanley's father, only telling him that he had died. The boy was charming and intelligent, and David enjoyed him thoroughly.

Later in the semester, David taught about righteousness, the gift of God. As he continued, he noticed tears dripping onto Cathy's, desk despite her attempts to wipe them away. After class, she left in a hurry, and he had to run after her to catch her. Her legs were no match for his long strides, and he turned her to him.

"What is it, Cathy?"

"I want you to quit coming by. Stanley is getting too attached, and there's no future for us."

"Why? Are you still married?"

"I've never been married. I never will be."

"That's foolish. You are a beautiful, vibrant young woman. I'm sure I'm not the only man attracted to you."

"Quit it, David. Let it go, all right?"

"No, it's not all right! I'm tired of this evasiveness. Tell me, Cathy."

"Okay, I'm a prostitute. I was raped, and Stanley is the result. Is that enough? Are you through?"

David drew the sobbing woman to his chest. When she calmed to sniffles, he put his fingers under her chin and looked in her gorgeous hazel eyes. He pushed her golden hair out of her face, soggy with tears.

"Tell me." He led her to a bench underneath a towering cherry tree, and its spring flowers fluttered around them in the soft breeze.

"I ran away from home when I was fifteen. I was on the streets, living under bridges; a woman bought me dinner, and offered to help me get a job. I wanted to go to college and needed to earn money. She said her boss could get me an ID, a social security number and a job. He did. At first, I was an escort, accompanying gentlemen to various functions, and then he told me there was more to the job than that. I lived in the house, ate their food. I had nowhere to go." Cathy looked down. "The first time, I was a virgin. The man was older, a widower, and he asked for me often, but he didn't...we didn't do that much, mostly we cuddled. He was Stanley's grandfather. I loved him, and he loved me—he was the first man who ever loved me in my life."

She took a deep breath. "But there were others, lots of others." She shrugged, looking away, avoiding his eyes.

"When did you come to Christ, Cathy?"

"It was a process. After I was raped by that older man's son, I ended up in the hospital. He beat me, ruptured my spleen, and did some other damage. The police came, and the prostitution ring was broken up. After a week in the hospital, I was discharged to a Christian mission. I was hungry for God and went to chapel every day. When I didn't have my period for a couple of months, they took me to a Christian pregnancy center. From there, I was taken to a Christian maternity home. In the kitchen of Hope House, with the housemother, Miss Ginny, and Beth, our social worker, I asked Jesus to be the Lord of my life."

"Cathy, you're a new creation. You aren't what you were. You are a child of God. Washed by the Blood and given the gift of His righteousness. Didn't you listen in class? Righteousness cannot be earned—it is the free gift of God."

She huffed bitterly. "I am what I am, but I'm going to give my son a good life. It's not his fault. He is a gift of God. Mom told me God is the Author of Life, and I realized He was there that horrible night."

By this time David's arms encircled Cathy, and she rested her head on his chest.

"So, you see, you have no future with me. Go find a nice little Christian girl."

"Too late. I've already found the most courageous, most wonderful, most beautiful Christian woman in the world. I love you, Cathy, and I want to marry you, and Stanley."

"You'll be late for your next class."

"I'm taking you home." He rose, took her hand, and drew her to her feet. He put his arm around her and led her to his car. That afternoon he learned all her secrets. Her mother picked up Stanley at kindergarten and took him home with her, and Cathy poured it all out—the months at Hope House, the trial, finding Stan in Chicago and Stanley's adoption. David learned why she could afford a house, a nice car, and a Wheaton education. She told him why she ran away from home and how she and her mother had reconciled.

"That's why I want to be a Christian counselor. I want to comfort others with the comfort God has given to me."

"I want you to come home with me, over spring break." She started to protest, but he put his finger on her lips. "You need to meet my mom. You'll like her. She'll love you."

"Stan was the first man who ever loved me."

David stood and looked down at her. "Smart man. We need to get Stanley. You ready?"

Cathy went to the bathroom and washed her face with a cool cloth.

David took her hand as they walked to the car. They drove the few blocks to her mother's. Stanley begged to stay, but knowing Cathy needed her son, David promised him a Happy Meal. She grimaced, but the boy shouted. His mother shook her head and led him down the stairs.

Audrey stopped David, holding onto his arm. "She's been crying." He indicated his agreement. "She's a good woman, my daughter. A brave, good woman."

"Yes, Ma'am. I get that." She looked at him and nodded abruptly. "See you soon," he said. "Tell Clyde hello." And he followed the happy sound of Stanley's chatter.

Taylor Valley Orchard

Stanley ran to the big windows in the airport, standing on tiptoe to see the planes. They were on their way to David's home, and Cathy was still not quite sure how. David was sneaky, the way he used Stanley—what little boy can resist the lure of riding horses and playing with barn kitties, much less drinking fresh apple cider?

David planned to rent a car, but his brother met him at the Seattle airport. Cathy was surprised when the two men embraced. Michael, a huge man—at least six feet and maybe six inches—lifted his "little brother" off his feet. Dave was over six feet, but slender, and his brother was broad and muscular. She wasn't surprised to learn he'd been a linebacker at the University of Washington. What astonished her most was his coloring—he was obviously biracial, and Cathy wondered if David's father or his mother was a person of color. After the effusive male greetings, Michael took Cathy's hand gently in his massive paw, and tousled Stanley's sandy brown locks. He held out his palm. "How're you, my man? Gimme five." Stanley slapped the palm as hard as he could, and Michael laughed, and added, "Up top."

When the second meeting of hands didn't faze the big man, Stanley asked, "Are you Goliath?"

Both David and his brother laughed and assured him he was not. He was David's brother, Michael. "Are all your brothers this big?"

"Nope, he's the giant of the family—that's why he stayed on the farm to help my dad with the orchard."

"Aw, Davie, I would have stayed if I'd been 5'7. I love that place!" As they walked to baggage claim, he told Cathy she was about to see Eden, God's Paradise. He tossed David the truck keys and hefted their luggage, but Stanley insisted on rolling his own Spiderman suitcase. After the big man swung the bags in the back of the over-sized pick-up, he tossed the little boy in there as well, telling him he could ride in the back with the luggage.

Stanley's eyes rounded. "Mama says I must ride in the car seat. We have to buckle up, you know."

"How could I forget that, my man? Of course." He lifted the lad out and carried him to the back seat, where a bumper seat awaited.

"You were teasing, weren't you Mr. Michael?"

The big man chuckled. "Smart kid. I have boys myself, Stan the Man, and Beatrice would have tanned my hide if they hadn't been buckled in car seats at your age." In answer to the boy's question, he told him his boys were eight and ten. Yes, he was older than Mr. David, who was the baby brother, and he would meet all the Taylor sons this weekend when they came down to meet the beautiful Cathy.

"My mom?"

"Yep."

"Why do they want to meet my mom?"

"Because we have heard amazing stories about the beautiful and brilliant Cathy."

"My mom is pretty, and she's pretty smart, too. She studies all the time. But mostly she's nice."

"This vacation we'll make her play." Michael regaled the lad with promises of hayrides and bonfires, horse riding and kitties.

"I was planning to rent a car—what are you doing in Seattle?" David asked, and Michael explained the farm business that brought him to the city—a part they needed right away.

Cathy listened quietly to the men and her son. She sat in the back of the double cab truck with Stanley. David looked back at her and asked if she was okay. She tossed him a quick smile.

"This loud brother of mine hardly lets anyone else have a word in edge-wise—but Stanley holds his own."

"What does that mean, Mr. David?"

"It means you are keeping up with the conversation."

"Mama's shy, but I'm not. My daddy was a famous businessman, and I'm gonna be one, too."

* * *

Michael observed the lad in the rear-view mirror. He was a smart kid, didn't miss a trick, did he? He shot a quick glance at the boy's mother. She was serious—too serious—and looked uncomfortable, maybe even close to tears. Seeing the boy striving manfully to keep his eyes open, Michael put his finger to his lips and cut his eyes toward the back seat. David looked and agreed. He put his arm across the seat, reaching for Cathy's hand, but she settled into the side of the truck for a bit of a nap herself, and the brothers talked quietly as they drove north.

The noise of the truck rattling across the cattle gate woke Cathy. They pulled to a stop in front of a huge red barn with Taylor Valley Orchards emblazoned in bold white letters across the top of the doorway. Michael opened the door to the back to lift the child out, but Stanley reached for David and cuddled into his neck. Michael's hands overlapped as they spanned Cathy's waist. He lowered her to her feet, making sure she was awake before letting her go.

"I'm awake, thanks." Cathy craned her neck to look up to his towering height, and the big man was brought to his knees by her beautiful eyes.

He punched his brother lightly in the arm. "You didn't tell the half of it, Bro. This gal is gorgeous!"

Cathy blushed and fussed with Stanley's suitcase on wheels.

"You're gonna scare the poor gal, Michael, knock it off."

A green Ford Explorer pulled up beside the truck, and two boys tumbled out—big for eight and ten, but not only was their father a big man, a statuesque ebony woman stepped out of the truck. Michael swept her into his arms and kissed her soundly.

"Quit that, you fool, we've got company."

Michael laughed. "Cathy, this is my beautiful queen, Beatrice, who rules me with an iron hand and makes me grovel at her feet."

Beatrice rolled her eyes. "Did this go on the entire trip? It's a wonder Cathy didn't hitch a ride back to Illinois. Boys, leave your book bags in the truck."

"Yes, Ma'am," they chorused.

From the security of David's shoulder, Stanley peered at the boys. Two dogs, barking furiously, streaked over. The larger, looking like a lab mix, jumped on the older boy, and a smaller Australian shepherd licked the face of the younger.

"Can I pet them, David?"

David got down on one knee and sat Stanley on the other. "You sure can, but don't let them knock you over—they're kind of rambunctious." Stanley reached out his hand and giggled as the dogs swept their tongues over it and stretched for his face.

"Who is he, Uncle David?"

"Josh and Ben, this is Stanley and his mother, Ms. Walker."

The boys bobbed their curly heads at Cathy but looked at Stanley. "Hey, Gram's got cookies and milk, wanna come?" Holding tightly to David's hand, Stanley followed the boys up the broad wooden stairs and across the porch. They slammed open the door, hollering for their grandmother.

David's mother hastened to the door, opening it wider to welcome her son and his guest. She was of medium height, and her delicate hair was purest white. Her blue eyes softened with love as she embraced her sons. Cathy stepped inside, blinking at the sudden change from bright sunlight. She saw three plates with cookies and three glasses of milk.

"I hope you don't mind if I fixed the boys a snack. They're ready for one when they get home from school, and with all the running they do, between work and play, they wear it off quickly and always eat a good supper."

"Thank you, Mrs. Taylor. It's fine."

"Obviously, this is Cathy and her son, Stanley," David said. "Cathy, my mother Anne Taylor."

Michael saw Anne's bright blue eyes soften as she took in her son's beautiful friend—no wonder his brother was smitten! But they knew the girl's history, and their hearts went out to her.

Anne held out both hands, pulling Cathy a few steps closer. "Welcome, dear. We're glad you came and brought this guy with you. He doesn't come home enough these days."

"You know he's taxing his peanut brain big time, trying to get the Phenomenally Huge Dumb degree," Michael teased.

"Michael, you're getting on my last nerve today," Beatrice fussed. "What's wrong with you?"

Michael straddled a chair, plucking Ben's cookie off his plate. "Aw, Dad," the boy complained, but immediately his grandmother replaced it, smacking her son's hand.

"Gotcha, Dad," Josh said.

Michael winked at his boys and stood to slip an arm around his wife's waist. "I'll behave," he promised, nuzzling her neck. Her eyes melted into black pools, and she laid her hand on his cheek.

Beatrice did resemble an Ethiopian Queen, but Michael introduced her as a teacher at the school the boys attended. At her suggestion, Michael carried the suitcases upstairs but he came back into the kitchen before Dalton Taylor stomped on the mat outside the back door, pushing the squeaking screen door open.

"I see the truck—the prodigal has returned." A blond man about David's height grinned, grabbed David, and pulled him into a bear hug.

"Hey, Dad. You're looking good."

"Back at ya, not so bad yourself. Where's...your, uh...friend?"

Cathy was standing behind Stanley's chair protectively, but the boy was horsing around with his new friends, enjoying himself. She was the one demonstrating discomfort, but she squared her shoulders and sent a brave smile Dalton's way.

"Good afternoon, Mr. Taylor."

"What's this 'Mr. Taylor' stuff? My name's Dalton." He crossed the kitchen as if to take her in his arms, but she put out a hand, and he shook it.

Peering into her eyes, he gave her a soft smile. "What's the matter, honey? This rowdy crew a bit much for you?"

She acknowledged his question with a curve of her lips, not quite a full smile, but almost. "I was an only child, Mr., uh, Dalton."

"Michael is the loudest, I'll grant you that, but Thad, Russell, and Gabriel will be bringing their families this weekend." Noticing Stanley, Dalton squatted by his chair. "Another boy in this house? I like having my boys home, and we did manage one pretty little girl—Thad's daughter is twelve. But then he started with the boys, Ed and Dan, and Russell has four boys. Gabriel's a bit slow, married late in life. What 24, Mama? He's got one in the oven. Don't know if it's a boy or a girl yet. Our odds, it's a boy."

* * *

Cathy feared she'd never keep them all straight, but David assured her later after she allowed Stanley to be carried off to the barn, some of his brothers were studious and thoughtful. He explained, "Thad is a marine biologist and Russell's an engineer. Gideon is a meteorologist with a Seattle TV news station."

"Odd mix," she noticed.

"Dad was determined we'd each pick our own fields. If a man loves what he does, he told us, he never goes to work a day in this life."

"This orchard looks like a ton of work."

"But he and Michael love it! They know every square inch of this property and every tree. They get up in the morning whistling. Are you settled in your room? I think Mom put you two in the room with twin beds."

"Tell me about Michael. Is he adopted?"

"I'll get you some binoculars so you can see his eyes—just like Mom's, same color, same shape. She'll tell you about it."

Cathy's mind puzzled over that information. "You want to take a walk? Maybe go see the kitties?" David put his arm around her waist, grateful she didn't pull away, and they walked toward the barn. He pointed to a big garden, already planted in neat rows. "Those are cold weather crops: cauliflower, broccoli, kale, greens. We hold off on the plants frost damages, but even snow doesn't hurt those."

"I've never had a garden."

"Gracious! How did you eat? We'll have to remedy that."

"I do buy from the farmer's market. We eat fresh vegetables."

"I forget you're rich."

She looked away. "I know what it means to be poor."

"I remember." He leaned and pointed past the garden. "See the green house on the hill? That's where Michael and Beatrice live." He tugged her hand. "I hear the kids."

She did as well—uproarious laughter and men's deep voices. The boys were sliding down a mound of hay, and Michael and Dalton were throwing them into it. "Me, too, Mr. Dalton." Stanley held his hands up eagerly. She held her breath as David's father gently tossed him and he laughed all the way down. "You wanna slide, Mom?" he called.

Chuckling, she shook her head at her son. "I'll pass."

He stood in front of her. "I'm getting kinda dirty, but Mr. Dalton says I'll wash up good," and he ran to stand in line for another turn.

David's eyes twinkled at his little buddy, having the time of his life. He grabbed him and climbed up a ladder to the loft. Placing him on his lap, he hollered, "Hold on!" and he slid all the way down.

"Did you see that, Mom? Me and Mr. David went all the way from the top!"

"I saw."

"It was cool, Mom! Can we do it again?"

"One more time, buddy, then we need to wash up for supper, okay?"

After the next slide, Stanley clung to David's hand as they crossed the yard. "That was the funnest thing I've ever done!"

"More fun than the zoo in Chicago? Or the museum of science?"

Stanley looked stumped. "Those are fun, too, but this was the funnest."

David swung the boy on his shoulders, and then he plowed his hands through his sandy hair. David winked at Cathy as she looked up at her son perched on those tall shoulders.

After supper and a bath, Cathy and Stanley went to their bedroom, but she never returned to the family room. He said good night to his parents and paused outside their door, tapping gently. She cracked it, and he whispered, "Everything okay? He's asleep?" They both glanced where he slept, and David grinned. "Big day for him, huh?"

"He was out like a light five minutes after I got him in here." Which meant she had remained by herself for over an hour.

"Listen, Dad, Michael, and I could use some help with spring clean-up. We have a rake Stanley's size that the boys all used, if he wants to come along."

"I'll ask him. Thanks. Night."

Michael's Story

Anne had the coffee made and was moving around the kitchen. David had filled her in on Cathy's history, hoping his mother could break through her barriers and overcome her natural reserve and the secrets she was hiding, because his mom, more than anyone, could understand her pain.

Stanley woke up cheerfully planning another day of fun and wanting to know when Josh and Ben would be there. He was disappointed to learn they were in school, and griped as he dressed. He was still unhappy when they went to the kitchen, but Anne made happy face pancakes with a chocolate chip smile. They brightened his own face considerably, and he turned the syrup bottle upside down, pouring it all over his plate and onto the tablecloth. Cathy was horrified, but Anne laughed heartily, saying it wasn't the first time and it won't be the last, and tablecloths wash.

"Are you ready to go outside with David and help Michael and Grandpa Dalton in the orchard?" Anne asked.

"Can I, Mom? Can I Mr. David?"

Dalton chucked him under his chin. "We have a rake that is your size, boy. We're counting on it. But it's a long walk. We'll have to ride you in the wheelbarrow. How would you like that?"

Stanley looked at his mother. "I dunno. I've never done that before."

"You'll like it. My biggest brother, Thad, used to ride me all around in the wheelbarrow," David told him.

Stanley stared. "He's bigger than Mr. Michael?" he whispered, his eyes wide.

Dalton chuckled. "Not in size, Stanley. Michael outgrew all of us, but Thad's the oldest, then Russell. Michael in the middle, and then Gabriel and David—David is our baby."

"He's not a baby!" Stanley protested.

"Grandpa Dalton means he is our last child, the youngest in our family," Anne explained.

"I'm the onliest. My daddy is in heaven. He saw me when I was a baby, but I don't 'member."

Anne approached him with a wet cloth. "Will you let me wipe your hands and face, or do you want Mama to do it?"

He tipped up his face and held out his hands—precious chubby fingers, his baby fat fast disappearing. Dalton reached as if to carry him, but he held out his arms to David, calling back, "Bye, Mom."

Cathy gathered the plates and cups, handing them to Anne to fit in the washer. "He's growing up too fast."

"Kids have a way of doing that. Thad's oldest is 12 now. Let's take a cup of coffee and sit on the porch." The lowered themselves on the glider and pushed off, swaying lazily in the sunshine. "Stanly seems fond of David."

"I worry about that. When we finish next year, he's going to miss him."

"Where do you plan to go?"

"Back to Columbus, Ohio. I have friends there. It's the closest thing to home I've ever had."

Anne waited—David had told her about Hope House.

"Where do your parents live?" David had told her about them, too, but she was giving Cathy a chance to speak for herself.

"I ran away from home when I was almost fifteen. I grew up in boarding schools. My parents divorced the year after I left, but since then my mother and I have become close—she's helped me with Stanley. She remarried last year, but they live nearby and Stanley stays with them a lot."

"David said Stanley's father was dead...?"

Cathy blew a breath. "He was adopted by his grandfather, who passed away within a week after he found us. I'll never have to worry about supporting him, but I'd rather Stan were here to help me train him. We never married, but he was a dear man."

"You're young and beautiful. You don't want to marry?"

"No."

"I'm sad to hear that. Several years ago, when Dalton was fussing at David to quit getting degrees and start his family, he told us he hadn't met the right one. Last spring, he called us and said he'd found her."

"Last spring?"

"He saw you studying, but you got away before he could introduce himself. He looked for you, and when you signed up for his class he called to tell us, and we've been given updates ever since—surely you know he loves you, Cathy."

"I've asked him not to."

"Ah, how does the heart know not to love? It follows its own course. Let's walk." Anne held out her hand to the younger woman, and they wandered through the trees. The fragrance of the white blossoms overhead filled the air with sweetness, and busy bees intoxicated themselves flitting from one flower to another. Anne kept Cathy's hand in hers as they meandered.

"Stanley adores him," Cathy said.

"And you? You don't find him attractive? A lot of girls have set their caps for David."

She sighed. "I try to guard my heart. I don't let myself think of him that way."

"Why?"

Cathy dropped Anne's hand and faced her. "Mrs. Taylor, I'm a prostitute. I was raped, and Stanley was the result." She shook her head. "He's a fine man, your David. I told him to marry a sweet Christian woman."

After a silence, Anne cleared her throat. "David said you asked about Michael. Michael was born the result of rape, too. I was assaulted one night after shopping late at the mall. The man dragged me into his truck, beat me, raped me, and dumped me out by the side of the road. I was almost dead when they found me, and I was in a coma for two weeks. I was in the hospital for four weeks after that—broken bones, torn vagina, black and blue, but the worst of it was I couldn't face my husband. I didn't want him to touch me." She smiled and glanced at Cathy. "That would be the 'for worse' part, wouldn't you say? He never gave up, Dalton didn't. He put lotion on my body and kept me turned to prevent bed sores—we had a hospital bed when I got home. I wouldn't even talk to him or look at him. He read to me, took care of the boys, and when we realized I was pregnant, I tried to make him take the boys and let me go."

"My God," Cathy breathed.

"He quoted Ruth to me...You know the verses." And they repeated them together.

"But—how did you overcome that?"

"My husband never stopped loving me. He said God had given life, and this baby was ours to love. God chose us for a reason, he said. Gradually I came to believe him. You know how it is—when did you start loving Stanley?"

"As soon as I felt him move within me."

Anne smiled. "God does a number on mothers, doesn't He?"

"Sounds to me like He did a number on your husband."

"He did. I wouldn't have anything to do with Dalton, physically, until months after the birth—it was a hard birth, Michael was a big baby, and I had to have a C-section, but Dalton would watch him move in my belly, put his hand on him and talk to him. He promised to love him, and he kissed my tears. 'Don't cry, Mama,' he'd say, 'God gives us grace for the journey.' When I talked about placing him for adoption, he didn't argue—he would have allowed that, I think, for my sake, but when he was born, the first thing Dalton said was, 'He's got your eyes, Annie,' and he helped me settle him on my breast. And as soon as I recovered, he started wooing me."

Go for
the Honey

Dalton and David's eyes were magnetically drawn to the two women walking slowly through the trees. The soft breezes showered white blossoms over them and teased their hair. Anne's soft white fluttered, and Cathy's golden tresses lifted off her shoulders. The father and son stood watching with reverence.

"The Taylor men and their women—you two are pathetic!" Michael teased.

"This from the man who 'grovels' before his queen," David rejoined.

Michael bellowed out a laugh. "I admit. I'm as helpless as you guys. You've been a good role model, Dad. You've taught your sons how to love their women."

"Isn't she beautiful? Forty years we've been together, and she's as lovely as the day I married her—more so." He put his hand on the younger son's shoulder. "You see them holding hands? Your mother has healing in her touch. You did well to bring her here, son."

"It was all I could do to persuade her. I confess I resorted to some underhanded tactics, tempting Stanley with the hay rides and bonfires, and the kitties."

"She's no prostitute!" his father said. "She's a wonderful mother and a beautiful, sensitive Christian woman."

"Fifteen, Dad, fifteen and homeless." A muscle twitched in David's jaw. "What kind of evil would take advantage of a child like that?" A look passed among the three of them.

"What's wrong, Uncle Mike? Go, go!" Stanley pounded on the sides of the wheelbarrow.

"You, Stan the Man, are a merciless taskmaster!" Michael picked up the handles of wheelbarrow and ran, Stanley's happy laughter streaming behind them.

"I hope—I pray—I can make her mine, Dad. So far she has kept me at arm's length."

"Your mother said she was raped?"

"Violently—not as bad as mom—but her assailant did beat her severely. She lost a spleen and was in the hospital about ten days."

Dalton pointed to a nearby wooden bench, and the men lowered themselves. "Mother withdrew after her horrible experience. It took a long time for her to come back."

"I always remember her with white hair, but in the pictures with Thad and Russell, her hair was light brown. Did her hair turn white then?"

"When she woke from the coma, it had started to turn. By the time Michael was born, she was totally white. But that wasn't the only change. She shrank from my touch. That hurt the worst. We'd always had a good physical relationship, but she wanted no part of me. I wanted to hold her, comfort her, but she was dead to me. Oh, I could turn her, put lotion on her to prevent bed sores—when she had a sore place, the home health nurse taught me to make a paste with Merthiolate and milk of magnesia. I'd daub it on her and cover the places with a bandage. I'd take a long time, examining the whole of her lovely body thoroughly—I probably made some places into treatment areas that didn't even need it." He arched an eyebrow and the right side of his mouth curved up a bit. "I loved her so much—and I wanted her, even as she swelled with another man's baby. I've always thought my pregnant wife was sexy. I don't understand some men who don't. She was lush and full, with the soft glow of motherhood an aura around her."

David glanced sideways. His parents' devotion had been the mainstay of their children's lives, but he was awed at the intimacy his private father shared with him this day. "How did you bring her back, Dad? Any advice for me?"

"I'll tell you what God told me to do. One night when I tried to touch her and she shrank from me, I was at my wit's end. I'd waited for her to be physically healed. Michael was a big baby, and she had a C-section. He was a voracious nurser, and we were up with him sometimes on the hour, never longer than two hours until he was on solid foods, but he was eight months old. We were getting some sleep, but for 18 months I found no admittance into the garden of my delights. I waited and waited for my wife. After she rejected me yet again and went to sleep, I slipped out of bed. She was taking care of the boys by this time, able to run the household, but she still wouldn't let me in."

Dalton waved his arm around the orchard. "I came out here, where I work with God and feel His presence. I was angry with Him that night, and I bellowed, 'What do I do? Show me what to do, God!' When I finished railing at Him, I heard His soft, still voice. I've never heard the audible voice of the Lord, David, but that night I knew what He said. He told me to obey His Word. He told me to go for the honey." He smiled and quoted Song of Solomon 4:2, "Remember? 'Thy lips, O my spouse, drop as the honeycomb: honey and milk are under thy tongue; and the smell of thy garments is like the small of Lebanon.' Go for the honey, son."

David stood and plowed his hands in his pockets. "But at that point in the Song, she was the beloved's spouse. We aren't supposed to awaken love until it's time."

"When do you want to marry that gal?"

David released a short huff of a laugh. "Almost a year ago. I saw her last spring, in the student center, and my heart stopped. I'm sure I've noticed other attractive girls, but she hit me like a ton of bricks. I thought *this is the one!* She was bending over her notebook, checking her textbook, and scribbling furiously. She wore her hair back, in a severe bun, but golden tendrils had escaped, and curled around her face. She glanced at her watch, and before I could go introduce myself, she ran out of the building. I know now she was going to meet her mother and Stanley. I kept looking for her, seeing her occasionally here and there, but last fall she enrolled in my honors class, and within two weeks, I was toast. She's not only beautiful, she's bright and insightful."

"I remember you called your mother and told her you'd met the one. We think you're right. She'll be a good helpmate for you because she has walked through the Valley. Go for the honey, boy, but you'll have to linger around the garden gate a while. Your mother and I will pray—and you know what happens when that woman prays!"

"I hope you're right—it's a big leap from a quick brush on her forehead." David stood. "Think we can interrupt them now?"

* * *

As Cathy and Anne ambled along, Cathy asked her, "How much does Michael know?"

"Pretty much all of it now."

"I've wondered about how much to say to Stanley. His birth certificate names him as Stanley Randolph Foster, Jr. I can confess to him he was born out of wedlock, but I don't want him to know about the rest."

"It was obvious to Michael, of course, but we let it unfold gradually as he was able to grasp the truth. He knew our teachings, our view of the sanctity of marriage, and he began to put two and two together. You became a Christian after Stanley's birth?"

"While I was carrying him. I was in a Christian maternity home."

They walked some more in silence, and Cathy felt Anne's hand reach for hers. She clung to it tightly. "Thank you for telling me. It must be hard to share."

"Not so much anymore. I wouldn't give anything for Michael, nor would Dalton. They're very close. They share the love of the land and a mystical connection with the orchard." Anne saw the men approaching and waved, a brilliant smile lighting her entire face.

Dalton's face split into a wide grin as his steps quickened. Taking her into his arms, he kissed her. "How's my Annie?" He held her tightly. "We saw two beautiful women coming toward us, and I thought old love is even better than young love." His lips brushed her hair. "I love you." His arms still circled around her, he rocked her a bit, side to side. They walked toward the house, their arms around each other's waist.

David blushed and looked at Cathy. "You and Mom have a good talk?"

"Thank you for bringing me here, David. I love your mom. Where's Stanley?"

David pointed. Up ahead, Michael was running, with Stanley on his back, beating him and crying "Giddy-up, horsey."

Michael swung the boy around front and lifted him high in the air. "Are you hungry, Stan my Man? Let's go see if we can find something to eat in the house."

David entwined his hand in Cathy's and lingered back, following the others at a distance.

He leaned her against a tree and brushed her lips with his own, then nibbled them and gently tongued them apart. She sighed into his mouth and allowed his sweet exploration.

"Will you marry me?" he asked when he raised his head.

"When?"

"Right after the semester. I'll start my dissertation in the fall, but I'll take the whole summer to love you, and forever won't be long enough."

She looked up at him. "You are a very handsome man. I just realized that."

"Took you long enough."

"Too long. I didn't look closely enough."

"To what do you attribute this closer look?"

"Your mother, of course. She told me many women had set their caps for you—is that true?"

"You know mothers—they exaggerate their children's looks and behavior. I've never loved anyone but you.

"Now, that's a likely story!"

He stopped and crossed his heart in the manner of young children. "It's true. I've been pretty set on my course, I'll grant you, but I've never looked closely at anyone until I met you. I love you and your son."

"Stanley asked me last night if he could have a daddy who lived on earth."

"Would you let me adopt him?" David asked as they proceeded toward the house.

"I don't think so. I told you his grandfather, his legal father, left him his entire fortune. I think I owe it to Stan to let Stanley carry his name."

"Are you open to more children?"

She smiled up at him, a real smile, accompanied by sparkling eyes. "We'd like a houseful, both of us. You're good with him. You'll be a wonderful father!"

"Can we make sure he doesn't feel different from the others?"

"I haven't seen Michael with his other brothers, but he appears to be a proud member of the family."

"He is—he's been a wonderful big brother. No one ever bothered us boys with him in our corner!" David regaled her with several accounts of Michael's protection of him and the others. He reached for the screen door.

"Don't you have any 10-W-40 in this house? This drives me nuts," David complained.

"This week is the first time we've could keep the door open—spring opened her arms for you two," his father said.

"I saw them sparking in the orchard, Dad," Michael tattled. "He must've learned it from you and mom."

"What's that, Mama, 'sparking?' Can I do that?"

"How old are you Stanley?" Dalton asked.

"Six. I'm in first grade, and I got to leave school before spring break because I'm ahead."

"Six? Well, maybe in ten years...," seeing Cathy's look, he amended, "or eighteen or twenty."

"That's a long time."

"Longer than Grandpa Dalton. He was sparking when he was seventeen or eighteen. How old were you when you got married?"

"You know perfectly well your father and I were married when we were eighteen—right out of high school, Michael Taylor!"

Stanley's eyes about popped out of his head. "Are you and David getting married, Mama? Is he gonna be my daddy-on-earth?" He bounced on his chair. "I love you, David. Can I call you Daddy?"

"Guess this is a done deal, then," Cathy replied. "I hope you didn't want any secrecy."

"Me? I want to shout it from the housetops." He ruffled the boy's hair. "How about you go with Mama and me to pick out a ring tomorrow? We want everyone to know she belongs to us, right?"

Stanley frowned. "Uncle Michael says lots of cousins are coming tomorrow."

"They won't be here until after school, buddy," Dalton assured him. "You'll go in the morning and be back long before they get here."

"Okay, David-Daddy. I'll go. When are we gonna make the cider?"

Dalton explained it was the wrong time of year to make cider—that would be in the fall—but they'd drink some cider and have a big bonfire Saturday night. "And this evening, we're going for pizza—how would you like that?"

Michael and David exchanged glances and said, simultaneously, "Tony's."

Cathy and Anne placed the last of the food on the table, a platter of sandwiches, potato salad, and chips. They held hands while Dalton said the blessing. Before long, however, Stanley began weaving ominously in his chair. David gathered him into his arms on his lap, and the boy was asleep in five minutes. He carried him to the bedroom, and they wrapped his to-be-eaten meal for later.

He didn't sleep for long, he was a big boy, after all, a first grader, but the fun in the sunshine wore him out. He gobbled up his sandwich, asked for more potato salad, and wanted to know when Ben and Josh would be home. Cathy took him to the tire swing in the back yard, and he enjoyed another new experience. Beatrice pulled in about 3:30, and the boys piled out of their car and rushed toward their new friend.

Anne saved his cookies for after school snack, and all three of them headed for the house, squashing together at the door in a huddle of giggles.

"They could hardly wait to get home," Beatrice said. "They were afraid you'd be gone."

"Dalton says we're going to some pizza place tonight, I hope they don't ruin their appetites."

Beatrice raised her eyebrows. "Tony's. He always takes her to Tony's—so she told you about Michael?"

"She did—but they love him so much, Beatrice! They both do."

"We know that—he was blessed the day he was born into this family."

"Amazing people," Cathy murmured.

Beatrice's many bracelets jangled as she reached for the door. Anne handed her a cup of tea, and she sat at the table with the squirming boys. "Did you tell Stanley about the baby goat, boys?"

Excited, the boys tumbled over their words to tell him about the goat, born last night at their house. Stuffing whole cookies in their mouths, they slammed the door behind them, running down the lane to the green house on the hill.

Michael anticipated their arrival and prepared three bottles of milk. They had another baby goat, about a month old, and he figured mama goat might take a bottle, too. He told Josh to handle the large goat and the two younger boys fed the small ones. Stanley had been too excited to tend to his bathroom chores and clutched his pants. Smiling, Michael put his hand on the lad's shoulders and turned him around. "See that tree over there? See if you can hit it. We live in the country, and the good part about being a man is the world is your urinal."

"Better not let Mom hear you say that, Dad," Josh warned.

"Don't get me in trouble, Stan my Man. This stays right here."

"Go ahead, Stan," Ben urged. "We do it all the time. Wanna see?" He provided a demonstration, and Stanley quickly caught on.

Grinning from ear-to-ear, he pulled up his zipper. "That's cool, Uncle Michael."

Michael's bright blue eyes twinkled merrily. "Shh—keep it under your hat."

Stanley looked down, wondering what he had to keep under his hat.

Chuckling, Michael added, "That means keep it a secret, okay?"

Stanley looked vastly relieved; he shrugged his shoulders and promised he would.

"Can we go to the pond, Dad?" Ben begged. "Wanna catch a fish, Stanley?"

"We can walk to the pond boys, but Grandpa is taking us to Tony's tonight. We don't have time to fish."

"Okay. You gonna give us lots of quarters so you can dance with Mom?" Josh asked.

"Yep."

"We can get lots of quarters when we go to Tony's 'cause Daddy and Grandpa want to dance with their women a long, long time," Josh informed his new friend. "Daddy says he has to keep the love machine fired up." He looked closely at his father. "Is that something we're supposed to keep under our hat, too, Daddy?"

Michael couldn't contain his laughter, but allowed as how Mom probably wouldn't like that, either.

"'Kay, Daddy." Pointing, Josh ran toward the green pond ahead. They walked around a long oval body of water.

Michael held out his hands, halting the boys. Blinking up from a soft bed of grass, a newborn fawn stared at them, attempting to rise on wobbly legs. When none of them dared to breathe, the fawn settled back down and lowered his head. A few minutes later they quietly, softly moved away.

"That was awesome, Uncle Mike!" Stanley whispered as he reached for his hand.

"Wow, Dad," Ben added.

Tony's

The boys bathed and put on nice pants and shirts. This was a special night. All the ladies put on dresses, and David eyed Cathy appreciatively as her golden hair spilled over her shoulders, and her skirt rustled against her shapely legs. Stanley took his mother's hand, and they walked through the door David opened. The boy noticed his soon-to-be Daddy kept his hand on his Mama's waist, and he grinned. He looked up, and David winked at him. He felt warm and secure. Miss Beatrice—would she be his aunt now? He guessed so—kept a stern watch over her boys, but relaxed when Uncle Michael put his hand on her waist.

The wait-staff knew this family and brought their drinks automatically, pausing with pencils poised over their pads to ask if they wanted anything different. Soon hot garlic and cheese bread arrived, and, before too much time, the steaming pizzas. Smaller pieces were doled out to the boys, and Stanley stared, fascinated, as he watched the men lift the triangles to their wives' mouths. What, couldn't they eat their own food? But somehow, seeing the couples' warm smiles, their eyes lingering, and the ladies' hands curling around the men's, he felt happy. He cut his eyes over to David and his mother, but they didn't do that—maybe it was a married thing. This family stuff was going to be cool.

After the boys were stuffed, Michael, Dalton, and David loaded them up with quarters and sent them off to the game room. Stanley scrambled after his friends, leaving his mom without a second glance. Wordlessly, Beatrice and Anne took their husbands' hands and followed them out to the dance floor. Dalton put money in the juke box, and the first dance, as always, was, "Just the Way You look Tonight."

* * *

David extended his hand to Cathy, and she stepped into his arms. He drew her close, and the perfume of her shampoo intoxicated him. This was heaven! She was an excellent dancer, and he wondered if it was part of her necessary skills. He wouldn't ask. She rested her head on his shoulder. *Thank you, Dad! And thank You, Father God. She needs to be loved and cherished. Help me do this right.*

"When Beatrice heard we were coming here, she asked if your mother had told me about Michael. Why?"

"Dad always brings her here after she shares that story. It drains her, I guess, and he wants to give her a night off. And when we get home...well, you watch."

"She said he wooed her back to him after the trauma."

"I asked his advice today, about doing that for you. He quoted Song of Solomon 4:11 about milk and honey under the bride's tongue, and told me to go for the honey."

"David..."

"Hmm?"

"I've never been kissed like that. Ever. It was the sweetest, most tender kiss."

"He said that's what God told him to do."

They walked back to the table while the others danced.

"I need to call my friend, Candy."

"She was in Hope House with you? She's married, right?"

"Yeah. Joe married her there. She was big—about seven months along. He wanted to marry her before Eddie was born so he could have his name on the birth certificate. Eddie's about six weeks younger than Stanley."

"After we get married, before school starts, we should visit them."

"I'd like that. You'll love Joe. He prayed to be like Mary's Joseph and not know her until after the baby was born. They were set to go on their long-delayed honeymoon, and she got shot. She almost died. She was shot in the femoral artery, and the doctors grafted a vein. So, he had to wait even longer!"

"How in the world...?"

Cathy told him about Joe's father, Scooter, and about the step-father who had abused and impregnated Candy. "She fussed at me when I talked about never getting married, and she promised me she'd help me when the time came—not if, she said, but when."

"Another overcomer. You have some amazing friends."

"I do, but now you're my best friend." To David's delight, she leaned and kissed him, but then she got embarrassed, seeing Beatrice watching and tugging Michael's hand. Michael stopped dancing and grinned. "Let's go gather the kids up," he suggested. They ushered the boys back while Dalton finished paying for the meal, and they walked into the chilly night air. Each man draped a sweater around each lady, and the boys rode with Michael and Beatrice. Dalton handed his keys to David and crawled in the back seat after Anne. The ride home was quiet. They followed Beatrice's car, which paused to drop Stanley off before continuing down the lane. David picked up the boy and carried him to the bedroom.

"When you get him to sleep, will you come back to the family room and sit with me?"

Cathy agreed, but before she got to the hall, Dalton swept Anne in his arms and carried her to their bedroom, calling over his shoulder, "See you kids in the morning." Cathy thought it was the most romantic thing she'd ever seen, and tears sprung to her eyes.

She pulled Stanley's collared shirt over his head, and he flopped on the bed. Smiling, she pulled off his shoes and socks and then peeled down his pants. She managed to get some pajama tops on him, but let the bottoms go. He could sleep in his underwear this night. He was already asleep. She kissed his forehead, but knew her son didn't hear her whisper, "I love you."

David looked up from pouring two cups of tea. They carried them into the family room. "You have the most wonderful family," she said. "I've never had family. I don't know how."

"You're a natural. Dad said you're a wonderful mother, and you are. Hang on, you're in for quite a show when they all descend tomorrow." David set his empty mug down and raised his arm. Putting down her half-full cup, she scooted under it. He curled a lock of her hair around his finger. "I remember the first day I saw you. You had your hair up in a bun, but these two curls had fallen. My heart stopped. You were the most beautiful thing I'd ever seen."

She craned her neck to look at him. "When was that?"

"Last April. I kept looking for you, but only saw glimpses here and there. When you walked into the class in September, I thought, Thank God!"

"You used Stanley most unfairly."

"All's fair in love and war, haven't you heard?"

She smiled and rested her head again, but her hand crept up to his cheek. "David?"

"Hmm?"

"Would you...would you kiss me again?"

He obliged. When he lifted his head, bright tears glistened on her lashes and ran down her cheeks. He kissed each one of them, tasting their saltiness. "I love you, Cathy, and I promise I'll be good to you and Stanley, as long as we both shall live. Michael was right. Dad's been a good role model. He has lived out his love and devotion for his wife before our eyes. I'm late to arrive to romance, but I'm looking forward to being a husband."

"I believe you."

He stood, rearranging his trousers. "I'd best bid you good-night. You need anything?"

"I'm good. Thank you, David."

"Thank me for what?"

"Thank you for loving me, and for loving my son."

"It's a pleasure—although, I must admit, more of one the last eight hours or so."

"Since you found the honey?" she teased.

"Definitely since I found the honey—more on that tomorrow."

In the morning David convinced Stanley to wait for breakfast in town. A wonderful café had excellent waffles, he promised.

"Where's Grandpa Dalton?" he asked.

"I believe he and Gram are sleeping in this morning."

"Mama says I'm a slug-a-bed when I sleep in."

David tugged on the boy's Taylor Valley Orchard ball cap. "She's generally right, but once in a while, it's okay."

"When I'm sick."

"Definitely, when you're sick."

"Are they sick?"

"Not today. Today they're just slug-a-beds."

"Slug-a-beds miss all the fun, Mama says."

"Not always." David grinned, winking over his head at Cathy, whose cheeks glowed with a pretty blush. She lowered her eyes. "Hungry?"

"Yes!"

"Let's go then." David grabbed the boy by his waist and trotted him to the car. Cathy grabbed the bumper seat off the porch and set it in the back. David leaned in and buckled it snug. "All set?"

"Yes, Sir, Daddy, sir."

"I like that, buddy—when you call me Daddy. Let's get Mama a ring."

"Breakfast first, okay?"

"Breakfast first," he confirmed. "God, I love that boy!"

"And my mama."

"And your mama."

"But you liked me before you liked my mama," he said.

"She's grown on me."

"Yeah, I can tell."

David chuckled. "I can't keep any secrets around you, can I?"

"I saw you kiss her, David. I mean, Daddy."

Cathy put her hands over her face. "Can we change the subject?"

"Mamas kissing daddies is a good thing, Mama."

"A very good thing, Stanley. I hope you don't mind," David agreed.

Stanley was quiet. David looked at him in the rear-view mirror, and Cathy looked over the seat.

"I like seeing Uncle Michael and Beatrice and Grandpa and Gram," he said thoughtfully. "I feel warm inside."

"Me, too, baby, me, too," Cathy agreed, and for once he didn't protest he wasn't a baby.

Knowing Cathy was a wealthy woman, David was nervous about the ring he could afford on his teaching assistant salary. He'd been a student a long time, but she didn't want anything too expensive. She picked out an antique-looking set, with a small diamond and a carved, broad gold band.

As Stanley slept on the way home, David apologized. "I could have bought something a bit more for you. Are you sure you like that one?"

She explained the things her father made her mother do to "entertain his business associates," and the things he wanted her to do. "I was home from school—I was barely fifteen, and he told Mom I was old enough to be 'useful.' He told her to buy me a dress, take me to the beauty shop and teach me what to do. He made me put my hand on the thigh of a drunk old man—one of his customers. Mother entertained another associate. He always bought Mom an expensive necklace or bracelet after she had to sleep with one of them. I hate ostentatious jewelry! After that night, I decided to run away." She shuddered. "Mom wanted to come to see me when the Hope House needed their signature to obtain custody, so he divorced her and said all the jewelry he'd supposedly given her was his!"

"A lot of bitterness there, Cathy?"

"Not really—I've got my mother. He doesn't. He lost, big time."

"I like your mom."

"I couldn't have made it without her." She described how Audrey had moved to Columbus and rented a three-bedroom apartment and they shared childcare while they both went to school.

David asked how she'd met Clyde, and Cathy explained he was Stan's butler. "When we came to Wheaton, we went to have dinner with the attorney in Chicago—you met him, Allen Overstreet. Clyde was there, and he was immediately attracted to Mom. He moved up to Wheaton and got a job overseeing the dining hall. They were married a year later."

"He was a butler? I can see that—he's polite and courteous. Definitely a butler-type."

"He was devoted to Stan but thought the worst of me."

"Why's that?"

"Look at the situation, a conniving young prostitute after the old man's money."

David took a deep breath. "I guess he thought the worst."

"He did, but he became convinced we genuinely loved one another during those few days we had before Stan died. I did love him, David. Does that bother you?"

"He was good to you, and you were very young, and essentially fatherless. I get it."

Cathy rummaged through her purse and pulled out a carefully folded piece of paper. She glanced over. "Stan was the first man who ever loved me. He wrote this before he knew me as Cathy. I had a false identification as Shirley Cooper, age 21. He had no idea I was only 15."

She began reading. "Dearest Shirley, I pray Allen finds you. I have upmost respect for you, my dear, and I want you to have sufficient funds to fulfill your dream of college. I want you to go to a fine school. You're a smart young woman, and you've been the best thing in my life. I appreciate you. I can almost believe you loved me, in a strange sort of way. We were an odd couple, Shirley. Thank you, from the depths of my heart. I've searched to find you and make sure you are well. I'm sorry beyond words for what Charles did to you. Be blessed, be happy. Love, Stan."

"I read that again last night and realized he wanted me to be happy. I am blessed."

David didn't have anything to say, and they rode in silence.

"Are you angry?" she finally asked.

"No. I'm not angry. I've never understood the need to...to hire love."

"He was a lonely old man. He'd been married for many years. He'd loved his wife, I guess, but they fought over the way she indulged their son, and her last years she was ill. It'd been a long time for him. He was..." Her voice trailed off as she fumbled with what she should say.

"He was kind to you?"

"He was. He didn't want much. Mostly we cuddled. He used to ask for me every time he came to Columbus. I was sixteen when his son...did that."

Mostly. God help me!" David reached his hand across the seat and took her hand. He brought it to his lips. When he looked over, she was crying again. He wondered how long she would cry.

She shoved her fist in her mouth and looked out the window. "What time do you expect your family?"

David approximated the time his brothers would arrive. "If you'd like to take a nap, I'll watch Stanley."

He turned into the drive as Stanley popped up. "I'm awake, Daddy David. Lemme see your ring, Mama." Cathy stretched her hand over the seat and he examined it carefully. "I like it, Mama. You make it pretty."

David opened the back door and lifted him out. Seeing Dalton appear at the top of the steps, Stanley ran toward him, raising his hands. Dalton swung him into his arms.

"Mama says slug-a-beds miss all the fun, but Daddy says sometimes they don't." Dalton looked over the boy's shoulder and raised his eyebrows at his son. "Were you having fun, Grandpa?"

"Definitely, my boy!"

"That's good, I guess, but I don't know how you can have fun in bed."

David turned around and walked back down the stairs. Cathy's face flamed, and she looked for a hole she could crawl into.

"Doesn't Mama ever tickle you in bed?" Dalton asked.

"Oh, yeah. That's fun. Were you tickling Gram?"

"You might say that. Was I tickling you, my Annie?"

"Dalton John Taylor, you are incorrigible. Now stop that!"

Chuckling, he leaned over the boy in his arms and planted a big kiss on her cheek.

"Kissing's fun, too, isn't it Grandpa?"

At that point, Dalton surrendered. "You are too much, Stan-the-man. Are you ready for the cousins to come? Do you need a sandwich before we make the bonfire?"

"I'm so sorry," Cathy apologized.

"Don't be. He's just an observant young man, aren't you Stanley?"

"What does that mean?"

"It means Grandpa talks too much!" Anne fumed.

"Really, it means you see a lot," Dalton corrected.

"I told Daddy I like to see you kissing. It makes me feel warm inside."

Dalton held the boy close in a fond embrace. "That's exactly the way God made it to be."

After everyone admired the ring and ate lunch, David took Stanley outside, and Cathy went to lie down. She tucked the letter from Stan into the side pocket of her suitcase, wondering if she should have shared it with David. As much as possible, she wanted to be honest with her fiancé—her betrothed—but she didn't want to hurt him.

Anne paused by the slightly cracked door. "Are you all right?"

"Come in." Cathy fetched the letter again. "I read this to David, but maybe I shouldn't have."

Anne skimmed through it. "Stan is Stanley's father?"

"Grandfather, but he legally adopted him. I don't know what to tell David. I don't want to hurt him. I know I've...done things I shouldn't have. I don't want to have secrets, but some things I don't want to remember." Cathy looked up into Anne's warm eyes.

"I blocked out a lot of things, and I didn't tell Dalton things that would create anger and bitterness. I spent a lot of time with counselors."

"I did, too, at Hope House. David is the one who brought me to an understanding that righteousness is never what we do, but what Christ has done—it's the exchange made at the Cross."

Anne walked over to the bed and sat. "Isn't it strange that we women take on the guilt of what men have perpetrated upon us? I guess not. Satan is the accuser of the brethren, and he torments us, doesn't he?"

Cathy sat beside David's mother and fumbled for her hand. "I'm sorry I stirred up old memories for you."

"I told Dalton last night the good that has come is the setting free of others. I've been able to share my experience with several other women."

"Comfort others with the comfort God has given you. I told David that's why I want to be a Christian counselor."

"You couldn't have done a good job until you were free to love and be loved, Cathy. God brought you David."

"He's been patient with me."

"He loves you—and you have received his love, hmm?"

"Yes, Ma'am. I've realized how much I love him, too."

Anne pulled her into her arms. "My sweet daughter. I love all my son's wives, but we share something I hope they never experience." She kissed her brow. "David said you were wrung out because of some things you shared. Can you rest?"

Cathy wiped her eyes—would they leak forever? —and nodded.

"Good. I'll leave you to it, but I'm here, if you need me."

"God brought me here. He didn't give me David. He gave me all of you. I was an only child in a loveless home, and the Taylor family is teaching me how to be a part of a family."

"You're an excellent mother. Stanley's a fine boy." Anne rose after squeezing the young woman's hand. "We're glad to have you in our family. Next time you come, bring your mother."

"And Clyde. He's been a good husband to her. He was a butler for years, and he treats her like a queen. After years of abuse, she's truly loved."

"I don't think I've ever met a butler," Anne said at the doorway. "Sleep. We'll make sure you're awake when everybody gets here."

Thad and his wife and four boys arrived early. School let out for the day, and they came in by mid-afternoon. Stanley, Ben, and Josh took the cousins to see the baby goat, promising to come back soon and play with the kitties.

Cathy stood at the porch door and watched them run off, screaming and racing. "Are they all right, David? Should we go with them?""

"Michael is down there, and Thad and Diane went with them. Did you get a little rest?"

"I've never seen him like this. Usually he hangs around me. I've hardly seen him since we've been here."

David searched her eyes. "Is that okay? He seems to be having a grand old time."

Cathy smiled. "He is. He's adapting rapidly to this big family. And, yes, I'm fine."

David stood on the ground below the steps, and once again she leaned forward and initiated a kiss.

"I love your kisses. They are sweet and soft," she murmured against his lips.

"You may have to hold off on those kisses for a while—unless you want to get married this week." She pulled back and asked why. "Because...well, because the kisses might be sweet and soft, but I'm...uh...hard and achy."

Cathy stepped back, losing her balance. He steadied her. "I'm sorry!"

"Don't be sorry. I love your kisses. But it's two months until the wedding." David tugged her to the porch swing and explained the first chapter of the Song of Solomon, where the beloved is advised not to awaken love until it is time.

"I don't know how—. Forgive me, David."

"I told Dad this would be risky—I thought you'd slap me, for one thing, and I knew how much I want you, but we must wait for the season of love."

"Candy told me to read the Song of Solomon. She and Joe read it on their honeymoon."

"After we're married and have some time to ourselves, let's go to Columbus so I can meet all your friends."

They sat on the swing, planning a wedding at Wheaton, and a honeymoon in Victoria, Canada—Stanley could stay at the orchard. They would go to Columbus later, in the middle of the summer.

Wheaton Wedding

David came into the house one afternoon after he picked up Stanley and saw a stack of books. Cathy grabbed them and carried them to her bedroom. She had called Candy as soon as they returned to Wheaton, and she sought birth control immediately. They planned to wait to start their family until they had finished their degree programs. The friends talked often, having lengthy conversations about marriage. David listened to them and heard Candy give her the titles of the books Beth had given her, which Cathy purchased and read over and over. Beth called as well, congratulating her on her engagement and learning about the courtship.

Cathy told him Beth told her she couldn't have been a good counselor until her healing was complete—and that included learning to love a man. "Your mom told me that, too, and God gave me you, David."

After Stanley went to bed, he asked Cathy if he could see the books Candy suggested. He thumbed through them before he went home, asking if he could read them when she finished.

Cathy and David married in the Wheaton College Chapel on May 25. Only Laura could come, and she was the bridesmaid. Beatrice and Michael were in the wedding party, Michael serving as the best man. They left Stanley, Clyde and Audrey with Anne and Dalton. After their honeymoon in Victoria, the couple traveled with Stanley to Columbus and spent a week at the Renaissance Hotel, where Candy and Joe spent their honeymoon. Candy and her wonderful, large family of Hispanic in-laws threw a reception for them, and David met Beth, John, and their families, and, of course, the beloved Miss Ginny. Michelle, who was at the University of Ohio, in medical school, came to the reception as well, and one day they spent with Laura, who was pursuing a degree in women's ministry.

Candy gave Cathy a haircut at her shop, telling her friend how Carlos and Juan had provided Joe and her their businesses in Conlos Corners. Stanley and Eddie got along famously and played games together on Merida's computer in Carlos's office. David loved Candy's Hispanic family, realizing God had provided healing for another one of His children by placing her in the middle of a large, loving family. Candy wasn't the abused trailer-park teenager Cathy had described, and his own quiet, serious wife was blossoming into a happy, playful woman. God certainly did all things well! When he mentioned that to Joe, Candy's husband shared how he, too, had an abusive father, and not only had the family been part of Candy's healing, Rod Rodriguez had been a father to him. God was in the restoration business, they concluded.

"But loving an abused woman has its rocky places. They misunderstand you because of their past experiences with men. When she gets distant, I've learned to pull it out of her, and usually I was totally unaware of what I'd done," Joe told him.

"I hope you'll tell me if you see me doing something wrong," David said.

At the end of their week in Columbus, Eddie and Stanley planned their next visit. "When you come back next year, we'll have a reunion and get Missy O'Malley over here," Candy exclaimed, wrapping her friend in a close hold at the airport. "You'll love Missy, David. She is the most spiritual person I know!" Joe and David shook hands—they shared the deep bond of loving abused women, and they had become quite close in a week's time.

Cathy and David buckled down after their summer of love. Stanley fell into the routine of second grade. His mother or grandmother picked him up from school and took him to soccer two afternoons and a reading club at the library every Wednesday. They attended church most Wednesday nights unless Mama or David had a big paper or a test. He loved having a daddy, and sought him out to discuss anything in his young life that puzzled him. David loved helping him with friendship problems—the bully at soccer, the 'mean teacher,' and the cute little girl in his class. Cathy bought him a game system and allowed him one hour each day to play on line with Eddie. Life settled into a routine.

By second semester, the couple was satisfied they were on target. Both should finish up by the end of the year. David's doctoral thesis was on track, and he felt confident it would be published. He would defend it in April, God willing. Cathy's internship would begin in February, and her thesis was on track to be completed in May.

David picked up the phone in his office. "Where's Cathy?" Audrey asked.

He looked at his watch. "She should be dropping Stanley off at soccer."

"The school called me. She's not answering her phone. I got him and took him to the field. I've been calling her, too, but I need to get back to work. This is my late day."

After hanging up, David grabbed his jacket off the hook. Cathy wasn't at the school, nor where she'd begin working in a few weeks. He drove to their home, heaving a sign of relief when he saw her car, but he fought mounting anxiety when he entered the quiet house. He called for her, and by the time he came into their bedroom, she was sitting, rubbing her eyes.

She looked at the clock and scrambled up. "I didn't get Stanley. I'm late. He's late for soccer. I can't believe this!" She shoved her feet into the shoes beside the bed.

David put his hands on her arms to calm her. "He's fine, honey. Your mother got him. He's at soccer now."

"This is her late day. I'm supposed to get him, but I fell asleep."

David sat on the bed and pulled her down beside him. "I need to call her. She was worried." He reached the phone beside the bed and told Audrey Cathy was fine.

"You've been tired a lot lately," David said. "We need to get you checked out. Maybe your thyroid is low or something."

"My thyroid isn't low."

"And you know this, how?"

"I know what's wrong with me." She burst into tears. "I'm sorry."

"What are you sorry for? What's wrong?"

"I'm pregnant. I know you didn't want to be pregnant." She wiped her nose on her sleeve.

"Pregnant? Wow, that's fabulous! Why wouldn't I want to be pregnant?" He touched her belly. "When did you find out? Why didn't you tell me?"

"I did a home test last week and went to the clinic this morning. You wanted to wait until we were finished. It happened because I was on antibiotics. Did you know the pill doesn't work if you're on antibiotics? I didn't read the prescription. It's my fault!"

"Seems to me God chooses these things, Cathy. Do you think He made a mistake?" Looking toward the ceiling, he added, "God, what are You doing? Didn't You know our best laid plans? Do You dare to give us a son or a daughter? Do you intend to make Stanley a big brother now, of all times? Whatever are You thinking, God?"

Cathy stared at him. Her mouth dropped open.

With his thumb and a finger, David gently closed it so he could kiss her. He pulled her down to the bed, brushing back her hair. "It's fine, sweetie. It will all work out."

"You're not angry with me?"

"Why would I be angry that our love has created new life?" He rolled over on top of her, looking in the hazel eyes that captivated him. "In fact, since we have an hour to ourselves and some unexpected time off, and we don't have to worry about getting any more pregnant, we ought to make use of this opportunity. Hmm?" And he slipped his hand under her blouse.

Cathy giggled and responded to him. He was a fortunate husband—she was a responsive wife and never turned him away. She was shy about initiating anything, but she made it clear she loved him, giving him her body unselfishly and enjoying his without reservation. Yes, he was a blessed man!

The family went out for pizza that night, celebrating what they decided not to tell Stanley for a while, but the boy was caught up in his parents' good mood. The next morning David spoke to his faculty sponsor, delaying certain goals because Cathy was tired, and he needed to pitch in more. He assumed all the cooking and shopping, so she could concentrate on finishing up by spring. The baby was due in late summer, and he wanted her to be finished before the birth.

* * *

Several weeks later, David was slicing and dicing when Audrey dropped Stanley off from soccer practice. "Game Saturday, right?" he asked the boy.

"Yeah. I'm headed for the shower. Where's Mama?"

"She's resting. Dinner's ready in about fifteen minutes. Shucks, make that twenty. I forgot to put the rice on."

Stanley perched on the stool and looked across the counter. "Daddy, what's wrong with Mama?"

"Why do you ask?"

"You do all the cooking. She rests all the time. And I hear her puking. A lot. Does she have cancer?"

David shut off the burners. "Stanley, she's fine. She's growing a baby, and when women grow babies, it makes them tired."

"We're going to have a baby?"

"We should have told you. I'm sorry you were worried."

"We're going to have a baby! Wow—how neat is that? I thought we were going to wait—you know, until you guys finished school. I'm glad we didn't wait. I didn't want to wait. I wanted us to have a baby right away. I'm going to be a big brother! And she's okay?"

To his credit, David didn't crack a smile about the 'we,' as if the boy had something to do with making the baby. "She's good."

"When?" Stanley asked.

"When is the baby coming?"

"Duh."

David bit back a response to the lad's fresh retort. They deserved it, after all, worrying the kid like they had. "August, probably."

"She's not gonna like that, being all fat in the summer, when it's hot. We should have planned this better."

"Sometimes God takes matters into His own hands." David turned back to the stove and turned the burners up, hiding his smile. He shook the Teriyaki sauce onto the stir fry. "Why don't you call her?"

Stanley hopped off the stool and ran back to their bedroom, hollering as if she was deaf.

Cathy took her place at the counter—when David cooked, they ate there instead of setting the table. "I hear we're having a baby," she said.

"Aw, Mama, you knew."

She chuckled. "I did, but we wanted to wait a while to tell you."

"I should know if we're having a baby!"

"You're absolutely right. We should have told you. We worried him, Mama. He thought you were sick."

"I'll be cured in seven and a half months."

"When our baby gets here. Daddy says probably August—I'll help, Mama. I'll get up in the mornings and get dressed. I can—what can I do? I can help fold clothes. I'll set the table, too."

And he did. Stanley became a big brother overnight, and Cathy said if she'd known how much help the men in her life would have been, she wouldn't have worried about being pregnant. The second trimester burst of energy occurred when she was writing her thesis and finishing up her internship. She finished on schedule and walked with her class at the end of May. It was an ungainly walk, but she walked proudly, her head held high. During the summer, she would gestate, enjoy Stanley, and make sure David was free to complete his degree, which he did by August. They all settled down to wait. David decided to teach a semester so they wouldn't be moving right after the baby came. Because of the trust, Cathy wasn't forced to work, although it bothered him somewhat that they lived in her house, supported by her funds.

When the time came, David gently shook Stanley awake in the middle of the night. "It's time, son. Your sister is on her way." Stanley popped out of bed, rushing around to get dressed. He pulled on mismatched socks, and his soccer uniform, which happened to be lying on the floor. Mama promised he could be in the birthing room! But it took a long time after they got to the hospital, and he dozed off in a chair.

Once again David shook him. Daddy looked tired, and his face was unshaved and covered with stubble, but he took Stanley in his arms so he could see. Mama looked tired and sweaty. She smiled and held out her hand. The doctor glanced his way briefly. "Not long now. Are you ready to meet your sister?" As he watched, the baby's little head slid out while Mama cried out.

Stanley took a deep breath. David set him on his feet and reached for the baby. With a grin as big as all outdoors, he put the baby on Mama's tummy. The doctor told Mama to push some more, which Stanley didn't understand. He thought for a moment maybe they had two babies, but he was fascinated with the one. He stared while a nurse handed Daddy some scissors, and he cut this rubbery looking hose. Audrey Anne cried then—really loud, too.

"Did it hurt her, Daddy?"

The nurse assured big brother it didn't hurt her—she was just getting her own breath for the very first time.

Mama was all smiles now, reaching for the baby, and the baby looked for Mama's milk, like the kitties at Taylor Valley Orchard.

"Are you all right, Stanley?" David asked.

Stanley bobbed his head. "I'm glad you let me see my sister be born."

"Let's go tell your grandmother and Grandpa Clyde." David reached for the lad and felt his fingers curl around his hand. The little fellow's hand was all boy now, and David thought about last summer, and the last vestiges of his chubby baby fingers. But he heard a child's excitement in his voice as he ran across the waiting room to tell all about the miracle he had seen.

After everyone had seen and held little Audrey, and pronounced her beautiful, Stanley went home with Clyde and Audrey and slept the rest of the afternoon. When they took him home the next day, Mama and Audrey were home, Daddy was shaved, and Stanley didn't want to go to soccer practice!

Mama suggested he call his friend, Eddie, who was expecting his baby brother in a few weeks. He took the phone, dragging a long cord behind him, and they heard his excited descriptions from the kitchen. "Don't miss it, man. Have you ever seen kitties be born? Oh, well, I guess it's kinda like puppies, too, only the mommies don't eat that gross stuff."

"I hope this wears off before he goes back to school," Cathy whispered.

"We'll have to explain it's not something we share with everybody," David agreed. "But he'll never forget." The baby began to fret, and David carried her back to the bedroom. "I'll change her and come back for you—we need to get you in bed."

With help from David, Stanley, and her mother, Cathy bounced back quickly. She enjoyed being a full-time mommy, taking Stanley to school and picking him up and tending to her baby. David had regular hours, except when he flew to various presentations around the country to present his research. In December, she watched with pride as he marched, wearing his robes with the colorful stole she had carefully draped around his shoulders. Anne and Dalton flew in for the ceremony, but left the next day to prepare for their Christmas at the orchard. Dalton thanked Cathy profusely for giving him a granddaughter and promised to spoil her, but, if she was like her mother, he said, she would simply be un-spoilable.

Because the college was closed for Christmas, Clyde and Audrey could join Cathy and her family on the Christmas vacation. When they arrived at the orchard, all the Taylors agreed with Dalton, who had proclaimed little Audrey an older version of Cathy. The wives admired Clyde, noting his tender care for his beautiful wife. The outspoken Beatrice claimed Audrey had been justly rewarded because of the abuse she suffered in her first marriage and Clyde was the Perfect Husband. "Hear, hear," the other wives proclaimed, while the Taylor men took exception to her remark.

"I was trained to be a butler, a single man devoted to the care of the household where I was employed. When Mr. Stan died, I was left adrift. He pensioned me well, but I was lonely, and when Cathy and Audrey visited the Overstreets, I fell in love, for the first time in my life. Imagine, a fifty-year-old man falling in love for the first time. I was foolish!"

Audrey patted his hand. "No, you weren't, Darling. You were precious. I was so far into my protective shell I don't know how you coaxed me out. It was your absolute devotion."

"I never understood how any man could refuse to be your slave, my dear."

Thad rolled his eyes. "Okay, Michael bows to his queen, and Clyde is a slave to his beautiful wife. I guess that makes the rest of us less than perfect husbands." He turned to his wife and asked if he could bring her anything? A drink? Snacks?

She laughed and asked for a kiss, promptly rendered, adding, "Please don't bring me another boy baby!"

"Can we try for a girl?"

The family was agog over the fair Miss Audrey Anne Taylor. Thad's daughter, Denise, a teenager now, carried her baby cousin around, rocked her, changed her, and would have nursed her if she could. Gabriel and his wife had produced another boy. Cathy found herself looking forward to another child and hoping the next one would be a boy so David would have a Taylor heir. Few people realized he wasn't Stanley's natural father, and Cathy knew he couldn't love the boy more if he had been his son by birth, but Stanley retained the Foster name. He had moved down the lane with Ben and Josh the second night they got to the farm, perfectly secure with Michael and Beatrice, who loved having him.

Denise brought baby Audrey to Cathy because she was hungry. "It's good thing I'm still nursing, otherwise I might never see my children."

David asked if she had a problem with that, and did she want him to call off the troops.

"No. They are being well-loved. Having all these cousins gives them a family." She brought her husband's hand to her lips. "Thanks for giving us a family, David"

"This galloping clan must be a bit much for an only child. We're all so accustomed to it, we don't realize how it must be for you."

"I always wanted a sibling." Noticing her mother blinking back tears, Cathy reached for her hand and squeezed it.

"I'm sorry, Cathy."

"I know. It wasn't your decision, and it hurt you, too."

Clyde was drawn to Audrey's side immediately and put his arm around her. Cathy realized her mother must have told him about the abortion.

"Did you have siblings, Clyde?"

"My father died shortly after my younger sister was born, and my mother did the best she could for her children. She put me into service very young as a houseboy. I sent money home to help her with the little ones, but I didn't spend much time with them."

Advised by realtors January was a bad time to sell, David taught again the spring semester, but he flew to Columbus several times to go over office plans with Carlos Rodriguez, who was adding on to Conlos Corners. They had a suite large enough for the two of them, and one weekend they flew together to go over the details, leaving Stanley with Clyde and Audrey. They looked around at some houses and returned to Wheaton to put theirs on the market.

Cathy worked on line with realtors in Columbus and showed David the printed photos and descriptions. He was less than enthusiastic about the beautiful offerings she showed him, and one day she confronted him, demanding what was wrong with this one, or that?

"It's too much."

"Too much what? It's not as big as the farmhouse."

"The farmhouse has been in the family for generations. It's above my pay grade, Cathy. I can't afford a place like that."

"But we'll have the sale of this house—which is totally paid for. At 25, I'll receive the entire inheritance that hasn't been put in trust for Stanley. We're trustees for his quarterly disbursements as well. We can afford this, David."

"You can afford it. I struggle with having your Daddy Warbucks support-ing my family."

Cathy didn't grow up reading Little Orphan Annie, so she didn't under-stand the reference. Rather than get angry with him, she bit her tongue and prayed. When she looked up the reference, she sympathized with his struggle, and she suggested they take three days to fast and pray.

David felt petty for taking away her excitement, so he agreed to a season of prayer.

The second day however, Audrey Anne was fussy when he came home at noon. Going into the kitchen, he prepared a can of chicken noodle soup and brought it into the living room where Cathy was struggling with the baby.

"What is this?"

"I'm not ready for you to wean her, and I don't think you want to either. A little soup is what you both need." He took the baby out of her arms and watched her dip her spoon, and he was struck with the sacrifice she was willing to make to come together on their decisions. "I respect your call to fast, and I'll keep on, but try a no-pleasant bread fast because of nursing."

"Okay."

Seeing tears hovering, he sat beside her on the couch. "This isn't a failure, Cathy. You're a mom. I can't stand it when you cry."

She gave him a quavering smile. "I guess I ought to give her some food, but I wanted to nurse her first so I wouldn't lose my milk."

Audrey cried herself to sleep, and David put her in the crib. He dropped down beside his wife on the couch, putting his arm around her and drawing her to his chest. "I'm doing fine, not even hungry, but I regret we didn't make love the night before this started—I miss your sweet body most of all. We haven't spent four nights apart since we married, have we?"

"Only when you've been out of town. I need you, too. You are so good to me."

"That's good to hear—I do okay as a husband?"

"Way more than okay." She leaned forward for a kiss, opening her mouth to admit him. "A little honey?"

He groaned. "Uh, maybe we can hold off on more of that."

She snuggled into his chest.

"I don't want anything to come between us, sweetheart. I'm struggling with being a provider—masculine pride, you know."

"I'm sorting through a lot of things...."

When she didn't add any more, he said, "One thing you should never doubt. I love you and the kids. I'm not going anywhere. Ever. I'll be with you whatever we decide."

"You're not only a good husband to me—you're a wonderful father for Audrey and Stanley. I didn't get pregnant to trap you."

David held her back. "Did you worry? It never occurred to me!" He looked in her eyes. "I could never lose you. Even if we never had children, I wouldn't leave you, Cathy. You are the other part of me." Hearing Audrey, he went to get her. "Speaking of her -."

While Cathy put her on the breast, David went to prepare the baby's food, but he was pleased to see the little one patting her mother, rubbing her chubby fingers across her mother's breast and sucking. Seeing him, she smiled and let the nipple slip out.

"Did I interrupt too soon?"

"No, she took both sides, and I did have more milk. Thank you."

"You're a fabulous mother. She isn't a year yet—she still needs that relationship."

Cathy asked him to carry the baby's food back to the kitchen so she could put her in the high chair. Glancing up at the clock on the wall, she reminded him he had a one o'clock class.

"I'm glad I came home."

"Me, too." Spoon in hand, she leaned up for his kiss.

"Careful, woman, you turn me on," he teased, and she blushed.

Doing more than pray, David sought counsel. He talked to his dad, and he called John, the Hope House counselor. All the wise men in his life agreed it was something to work out together, but Clyde was the most help. David took off early one afternoon when his father-in-law was off and went by the apartment. After he explained his struggle, Clyde leaned back on the couch and closed his eyes briefly. He leaned forward and spoke.

"David, the old man loved that child. Mr. Stan knew she would be at the trial to testify, so he sent Mr. Overstreet there. When he located her, he told Mr. Stan she was recently 16 and had given birth to his grandson. He was horrified to realize she was only 15 when that evil Donnie brought her to him. Mr. Overstreet brought her Chicago to see him before he died, and he wept, learning she was a child. She had an ID saying she was 21, and they made her appear older, but he thought what he had done was unforgiveable. Then she came—such a brave young mother—not only with forgiveness, but also with tenderness and with real affection. His drugged-up son had beaten her, raped her, put her in the hospital, and yet she carried the baby. We all thought she was remarkable—and Stanley does look like the old man."

"Allen told me that, too," David replied.

"Mr. Stan wanted to make it up to her some way, and he was determined to do right by the boy. I was in the room to witness the papers they drew up. He told Mr. Overstreet she was young, but wise beyond her years and he trusted her to make good decisions. Allen suggested delaying the inheritance until her 25th year, but he only agreed after writing out a generous check for her college expenses."

"But that's her money."

"Don't be proud, David. She's never could give in her entire life. First her father, and then that man, Donnie, dominated her, abused her, and controlled her. You have given her self-worth and devotion—what price can anyone pay for that? Talk to her, but with an open heart. She wants to give her son the best."

"Tonight, we break our fast and we'll talk then. Thank you, Clyde. You've given me a lot to consider. I have the rest of the afternoon free—I'll go to my office and listen to God."

"For what it's worth, I don't think she'll throw away God's gift. I believe God has brought you together, and you'll do good things for the Kingdom. She has dreams of a foundation, you know. She's talked to Allen about it."

"I wonder what else she's kept from me—she still has secrets."

"She still has pain."

"Pain?"

"Yes, pain, shame, and scars." David embraced Clyde, who added, "We'll pray. You've been the best thing in her world—you and those children.

God's Provision

That night Clyde and Audrey were at the house when he let himself in. Stanley was jumping up and down. His grandparents wanted to take him to see the latest Pixar movie! Mama was packing his overnight suitcase.

David chuckled. "I thought we were taking you Sunday."

"Please, Dad? I'll go again."

David laughed then. "Go ahead. It's Gram's turn." He put his hand on the boy's shoulder and carried his suitcase out to their car. Winking at Clyde, he mouthed his thanks over the boy's head and waved as he turned back to the house.

"What is this wonderful aroma, Wife?"

"It's a bland first meal, mashed potatoes and baked chicken. Are you hungry?"

"How long before Audrey Anne wakes up?"

"I took her to the park today. The fresh air tired her out."

"Can you turn the meal down without ruining it?"

She did, right before he swept her in his arms and carried her to their bedroom.

"You taste better than food," he proclaimed later. "But I've worked up an appetite. I'm hungry for the first time since Tuesday."

Hearing the baby, Cathy detoured to get her, and he promised to set the table. The table was set, but David must have left something in the car—the door was standing open and when he came in, his face was hidden behind the largest basket of flowers she'd ever seen. He placed it on the center of the table, right beside the candles. Not only was their food on the table, Audrey's was prepared and waiting on her high chair tray as well. Audrey screamed joyously and flung herself at her daddy.

"My two beautiful girls," he said with a grin. He sat and took Cathy's hand to pray.

After they finished the meal, he stacked the dishes in the sink, and joined her in the living room as she nursed Audrey. He retrieved the baby's toy-blanket and shook it out, laying it on the floor at their feet.

Cathy put the baby down and sat beside him. "Who first?"

"What has God revealed to you, anything?"

She lifted her chin bravely, but it quivered. "I'm sorry I've thrown my past in your face. I'm sorry for reminding you I was a prostitute. I don't know what to do. I've talked to Allen about a foundation, but I'd like to direct it, with you, of course. I don't need that house, David. I need you."

David shut his eyes. *Clyde was right. She does have pain and shame. I've brought all this on her. Father, forgive me. Help me to heal her scars.* He opened his eyes and saw her stricken face. He pulled her to his chest. "I didn't hear that at all, Cath. God told me to buy that house. He needs it for our work in Columbus. And, for the record, one more time—I never think of your 'past.' I think of the brave and beautiful woman I married who gave Stanley life, who forgave those who stole her childhood, who has given me two beautiful children. Please, honey, please believe me. God, help her to believe me. I honor you, baby, more than anyone I've ever known—you and my mother." And then he was busy, kissing away her tears. She knotted her fist in his shirt and sobbed. He'd made her cry, again.

When she was spent, he handed her a fistful of tissues, and she blew her nose. "What work in Columbus?"

"I don't know, but I see God's provision—not any man."

"Allen told me Stan knew I'd do good things with his money. Allen said he warned him money could destroy, and I was awfully young. Stan said it wouldn't destroy me. He said I was...good...through and through." She sniffed.

"We agree on that—you are, Cathy. You're a good person, and God will direct us in the use of the money. Will you fly down to Columbus with me tomorrow? I don't want to let you out of my sight."

"How long will you be gone?"

"Spring break starts. I don't have classes for a week, but I planned to come back Tuesday. Carlos sent me drawings of our offices—they're in my briefcase."

"Can we bring the kids?"

"Let's get on the computer."

They couldn't get seats together unless they switched to first class, but for the first time, David was fine with his wife being a wealthy woman and made the change, adding until the weekend since he'd have his family with him. Cathy called the real estate agent and set up a time Saturday afternoon. Then she called Candy, who was so excited David could hear her squeals.

Between the two of them, they packed suitcases for everyone. David rocked Audrey to sleep and led his wife back to the bedroom. "I'm well fed, strengthened, and ready for desert."

"Hmm, what did you have in mind?" She put her arms around his neck and pulled him down for a deep and lingering kiss. "Besides honey?"

He showed her.

The next morning, David called Stanley. "Hey, bud, Mom and I decided last night to take you and Audrey with us to Columbus. Eddie can't wait, your suitcase is packed, but we need to pick you up in an hour to get to the airport. Have you eaten?"

"I don't care. Yes, I have. Gram made waffles. I can be ready." He slammed the phone down, but not before David heard him hollering the plan to his grandparents.

Since they were ready, they locked up the house and went over to the apartment. David lingered in the kitchen with Clyde, who was finishing up the dishes, and told them they were looking at the house.

"Thanks, man, you got to me, and you were right on. Have you two decided to stay here or do you want us to look around for a place for you, too?"

"Audrey and I decided it was up to you two. We love being grandparents, and Cathy wants to use her degree, so we wondered if we could be a help." He dried his hands on a towel. "But you have your own lives to lead. It's my responsibility to provide for my wife's happiness."

"It's hard loving an abused woman, isn't it?"

"In some ways, yes. It's a never-ending job, but they're so grateful for the least little thing, don't you know?"

"We'll look. Cathy will send back some pictures, and you tell us what you like."

"Anywhere not too far from those children," Clyde assured him.

Joe and Eddie picked them up at the airport. Candy was working. Eddie told Stanley he was going to spend the night with him, and his mom and dad would stay with Aunt Merida in the Carriage House behind Uncle Carlos.

"Eddie, you need to clear those plans with Stanley's parents," Joe advised.

"We didn't have the kid last night, Mom, do you think you can take another night?" David glanced into the back seat.

Cathy, squeezed in between little Rod's and Audrey's car seats, glanced in the back row where two anxious boys awaited her response. Intending to tease them, she began thoughtfully with an 'I-don't-know,' but their pleas brought her laughing assurances.

"We're out for spring break, Eddie. Do you have school Monday?" Learning he was out, too, she granted permission for Stanley to spend the week at the Longs, and the boys slapped their hands in joyous high-fives.

"Do you think you can take this, Joe?" David teased.

"We can. We have a guest bed in Eddie's room for company. Candy and I had plenty of privacy when Martha and Rod were there. I may suffer a bit of deprivation, handling these two rowdy boys, but you guys..." He winked. "Enjoy!"

David reached to the back to take Cathy's hand. "We can make up for lost time!" He raised his eyebrows and grinned.

"We set up the pack-and-play. How old is Audrey?

"Nineteen months," David replied.

"She won't crimp your style then."

135

"Would you males quit your strutting?" Cathy fussed. Fortunately, the boys in the back were focused on some hand-held game system.

Joe pulled in at Conlos Corners. "Carlos said to bring you by first thing. We're gathering for dinner at his place, and you can unload your baggage then."

Candy was locking up when they pulled in, and the men were left to collect children while the women embraced. Candy sent her brother-in-law a quick text and led them through a walkway to the back row of offices. "He said to go on in—he's manning the grill—I'm to take notes of any changes you want, your colors, and if you want him to pick out drapes."

Pushing open the door, she ushered them in first. David had told her how nice the offices would be, but Cathy was thrilled. She had a small office on one end and David's larger suite was on the other end. A large conference room separated the spaces. She slipped her hand in his as he led her around. Her eyes sparkled, and he pulled her to his side.

"Like it?"

"I'm very impressed, Dr. Taylor. I'm sure you'll do well in this magnificent office. Don't you love the built-ins?" She waved her hand toward the walnut bookshelves along the back wall.

"I added those. I'll put my desk in front, and all I have to do is swivel my chair around to reach into my library." She put her arms around his waist and squeezed him. "I see one major problem," he said, with all seriousness.

Candy poised her pen over a small notepad.

"How am I supposed to stay focused on my work with this beautiful distraction in the same office?" He dropped a kiss on her forehead.

"I'll be right here to protect my interests when some unhappily married woman comes in and sees my handsome husband!"

"Doesn't look like you have much to worry about, Cathy, he's obviously a one-woman guy," Joe assured her.

"You got that right," David rejoined. "She's the first woman I ever loved, and she'll be the last."

"All right, you lovebirds, look at the bathroom and the kitchenette so we can get to the party," Candy said. "Since we have more days, you can pick out bathroom fixtures, and my sister-in-law's husband has a floor covering place in the Corners—hardwood, carpet, laminate, whatever you want."

With a grin, David asked if she knew anyone who sold fixtures so they could select their lighting. Joe punched him in the arm, and the men laughed. "Let's get out of here, Taylor."

"Right behind you, Long. How is your electric business coming?"

Joe told him he was expanding, taking up the space afforded by the new back row. "I can run down there before we leave and bring some catalogues for you two to look at."

Candy linked her arm in her friend's. "I'm glad our husbands get along so well. It's going to be great having you guys here! When you put it off, I was afraid you wouldn't come."

"I hated moving farther from David's family, but he said if you have to fly, what difference does it make? Mom and Clyde are coming, too. I don't know how I would've made it without them, and Stanley and Audrey adore them. I can't wait for you to meet Clyde—he's a kick. He was Stan's butler, you know, and he treats her like she is a grand lady."

"How wonderful—it's what she deserves, Cathy."

"Mom," Stanley stuck his head in the door, "Audrey wants you."

While Cathy changed Audrey's diaper and nursed her, the men walked down to Joe's shop and looked at fixtures. David put his hand over his eyes and peeked into John's floor covering dealership. As Cathy was buckling Audrey into the car seat, the husbands returned.

Looking backward, Joe winked at Cathy. "Steaks are calling me." He put on the brakes. "You boys shove over and give Stanley's mother room, Eddie."

"Yes, sir." Eddie bumped Stanley with his behind. "Shove over." They giggled and piled close to one another, leaving half the seat for Cathy.

Biting back a chuckle, Joe said, "I hope I can take it this week. I may have to strangle them."

"They'll settle down. They're glad to see each other," Cathy assured. "You guys want to come with us tomorrow afternoon to see the house we're looking at?"

Saturday afternoon, they met the real estate agent at the Longs. Cathy and David rode in her vehicle, saying little. They turned up a long lane, bordered by weeping cherries.

"These trees are not productive, Dr. Taylor, but the trees in the back are, and can be more so, with care. The elderly man who's selling didn't maintain them the last few years." The agent pulled to a stop and walked behind the house, pointing out the abundance of fruit and nut trees.

David looked down at his wife. "You bought me an orchard."

"A little one." She looked up at him. "You like it?"

"What if you don't like the house?"

"I like it." Holding hands, they followed the agent inside. Two boys barreled out of the Long's car and ran around the yard. The huge living room was dominated by a stone fireplace stretching across the back wall. To the right was the formal dining area, and off that a farmer's kitchen, with glistening granite countertops and storage for many units of canned produce. "In the basement is cool storage," the agent informed them. "The master suite is down the hall, with four bedrooms upstairs."

"Mom," Stanley cried, "where are you?"

"In here, Son," she called from the downstairs bedroom.

"Gosh, this is awesome, Dad. Do you like it?" Stanley found them. "Good grief, look at this bathroom! It has a shower and a tub. Does that tub have jets? Can I get in it?

The agent laughed. "Have you been on the deck? You'll find a hot tub there."

Stanley ran down the hall. "Let's find the deck," he hollered. Joe opened the French doors off the family dining area in the kitchen.

"Awesome," the boys exclaimed. They danced around the large deck overlooking the orchard.

"Maybe you want to see the upstairs. You might not like your bedroom," Joe teased the boy.

The boys catapulted up the stairs. The bedrooms were huge. Another master suite was at the end of the hall, and Cathy decided they would use that one until the children were older and put Clyde and her mother in the downstairs suite until they found a house.

"I have your retainer, Mrs. Taylor, but I didn't tender your offer. I recognize you're able to pay the asking price, but he's willing to come down. You'll have expenses in the orchard, getting it into shape, and maybe you'll need to have work done on the hot tub. The drapes need to be replaced. He expects to negotiate."

Candy and Joe sat on a bench on the deck during their friends' discussions with the agent. Joe was doing well, and his business was growing, but he couldn't provide for his wife like this. Candy leaned her head on his shoulder. "Did you know Beth had to find an attorney to make Cathy's father pay child support until she was 18? I'm glad for her. She's been through so much."

Joe thought about the foul trailer where Candy suffered her own years of abuse. "You girls are amazing. I'm really proud of you, Candy." His wife rejoiced with her friend, not even comparing this grand place to the little brick house they now owned down the street from Martha and Rod.

"I'm proud of you. I told you you'd be the best electrician in Columbus!"

"When are the stations going to be ready for your spa?"

"I've hired two estheticians and two nail people. We should be ready in a month, and they'll be able to start." They stood as David walked out, looking for them.

"Ready to go?" he asked.

As they walked into the living room, they heard Cathy inquiring about a place for her mother and Clyde.

"How much property is here?" Joe asked. "Any room to build?"

"The entire property is fifty acres. Several places would be suitable," the agent replied. "I'll have the Taylors the key soon, but you can walk the property any time."

"Juan can build them something, Cathy. Want to ask him? Heck, this place is easily big enough for them to stay with you until it gets done."

By the time they left on Friday, they had picked out flooring for the house and the office, selected shutters, measured for drapes and chosen the materials, even selecting the wall paints for house and office. David tucked the house plans Juan had given them to take to Clyde and Audrey, and teased about the Rodriguez family making a killing off them. But he was well-aware they'd be getting rock bottom prices on everything. They collapsed on the plane Friday afternoon, Cathy complaining they hadn't gotten much vacation.

David whispered in her ear, "The nights to ourselves were amazing." He tucked a straying curl back and let his hand linger on her cheek.

She blushed. "Hush!" but she took his hand, and her answering smile said it all.

The Move

Davie was pleased when Stanley, who had been having reservations about leaving his school, his soccer team, and their church, started marking the days off the calendar. In Columbus, Eddie had a party for him, took him to Sunday school, and of course he was with all the Rodriguez cousins—some of the girls were totally cute, he told his mother.

"How old is that kid?" David teased.

"He'll be eight in October."

After choosing a lot for their house from the photos David brought back, Clyde and Audrey selected house plans—they had to have at least three bedrooms to accommodate boy and girl grandchildren, and they wanted a screened porch with an overhead fan. Their wants were simple. Clyde told Cathy since they'd both worked in Columbus, his pension had accumulated, and he could buy the house, but he thought they might retire, live on his pension, and be available for the children.

"I owe you for the endless hours of childcare!"

"No, my dear, we owe you for giving us a family."

She hugged him. "I love you, Clyde."

He blinked, held her briefly and replied he loved her, too.

They day arrived, and both households were packed into one moving van. David discovered Cathy was pregnant again, and he refused to let her lift a finger—since her head was in the toilet most of the mornings, it wasn't too feasible anyway.

"How did this happen?" she moaned.

"Beats me. Have you been looking under cabbage leaves again?" David teased.

She looked up, took the warm washcloth he offered, and said, "You aren't the least bit funny."

"Sorry, baby."

"You should be! You did this to me."

"I can't help it. You're beautiful and delicious." He helped her stand. "I'll fix you some ginger tea." The next day they started for Columbus, her barf bag in her lap.

David thought this was worse than when she carried Audrey, Cathy looked terrible. The kids cried, "Eww!" every time she had to use the bag. After stopping to air out the car several times, he pulled into a hotel.

Clyde pulled in behind them, and David explained she had to rest. The grandparents brought the little ones in to their room while Cathy showered and then the older couple decided to take the children to dinner.

"I should have put you on the plane—I could have gotten you there in an hour," David fussed.

"Did you want to take these kids by yourself in the car? Because I couldn't handle them by myself on a plane."

"I'm sorry, honey." He handed her a cup of ginger tea and a handful of crackers.

"I seem to get pregnant at the most inconvenient times! I feel awful about the car."

David grinned ruefully. "The price I pay for fatherhood. I'll be back. I need to run out and get something to clean it out."

The second day they remained in the motel until her stomach was settled, leaving close to noon. Although the driving didn't help, she didn't throw up again, and they pulled into a hotel in Columbus by late afternoon.

The next day, David met the moving van at the house, insisting she stay at the hotel and let Clyde bring her out later. Audrey took the kids and went with David, so when Clyde and Cathy arrived, everything would be in place. A ten o'clock, however, David's phone rang.

"I'm taking Cathy to the hospital. She's miscarrying. Do you know where she delivered Stanley? Right now, she's lying on the back seat of my car. Wait, she told me. We're leaving."

David hollered for Audrey, explaining he had to meet them at the hospital and ran to his car, backing out and throwing gravel from the driveway even before his door was closed. "Call Candy to help you with the movers," he shouted out the window. He knew Audrey would take up directing them, and he prayed.

David was in the waiting room when Audrey called to tell him Candy had loaned her a car and she was on the way. Candy was directing the movers.

By the time Audrey arrived, Clyde told her Cathy was in surgery, having a D and C. The baby was dead. David sat on the far end of the waiting room, his head in his hands between his knees.

"Did you get to her in time?" Audrey asked her son-in-law.

"She knows I'm here. I walked her to surgery."

Audrey sat beside him. "I'm so sorry."

"She'll blame herself."

"David, these things happen."

"I know, the doctor told her, but I know her. She'll blame herself."

"Oh, God, help us to help her. Call Beth, David."

He mutely handed his mother-in-law Cathy's phone, and she scrolled through the contacts until she found the Hope House number. Walking across the room, she reached Ginny and told her what was happening. They promised to pray.

Audrey turned in a circle until her eyes rested on her husband, who immediately came to her side and took her in his arms. She leaned her head on his chest. "Why, Clyde? She's had too much pain. David says she'll blame herself."

"I couldn't comfort her at all," Clyde said. "She sobbed and sobbed. They had to give her something to calm her down, poor little thing."

When the surgeon came out to talk to them, he said the baby had died several days ago, but the good news was they had stopped the bleeding and her womb wasn't damaged. They could have other children. He allowed

David to go into recovery with her, and she opened her eyes to his beloved face.

"I'm sorry. I lost our baby I wanted to give you a son."

He leaned and kissed her forehead. "I have you, and we have Stanley and Audrey Anne. We'll leave this little one in our Father's hands."

"Can we bury him? Was it a him?"

How could he tell her they had nothing to bury? He shook his head.

She screamed.

The nurse hurried over as David tried to restrain his wife. The doctor retuned immediately and ordered a sedative to put her to sleep.

"She's taking this hard, but she's young and healthy, and she'll have more babies," he told David. "She kept saying it was her fault, and I told her it was no one's fault—these things happen sometimes, and we never know why."

"Doctor, I know you were called in on this emergency and you don't know her history. Let me tell you about my wonderful wife." The doctor could not believe the story he heard—a fifteen-year-old lured into the sex trade, raped and beaten within an inch of her life, and carrying the baby. David concluded, adding, "I knew she'd blame herself. That's what she does."

"My God! Listen, Dr. Taylor, I'm a Christian, and, obviously, you and your wife are, too. We'll see her through this. Let's pray," and the good doctor prayed. He stood and squeezed David's shoulder. "We'll move her up to her room. I'll gradually reduce her dose, but I recommend a Christian counselor—besides her husband." And he recommended John Morgan, the therapist from Hope House, because he'd seen a lot of abused girls.

David shook his hand. "We've already called him. Cathy was in Hope House when she had her son, and she loves John."

"He's the best."

"I've met him. He's a good man."

"I'll be keeping a close watch. Don't hesitate to call."

Cathy slept on the gurney as they rolled her into the room. Audrey stood beside the bed, and Clyde stood behind her. Cathy opened her eyes and turned her head away without saying a word.

"She'd want you to be with the kids, Audrey. I know Candy's with them, but that's what would make her feel better, right, honey?" She nodded. "I'll keep you posted," David assured them. She reached for his hand and clung to it.

Clyde gently tugged on Audrey's hand and led her out the door.

David had no success reasoning with her. She was convinced the loss of their baby was her fault.

At the end of the day, Dr. Reynolds entered the room. He crossed his hands over the clipboard in his hands and sat on the edge of the bed. "I need to ask you a few questions to be sure your history is correct." He looked directly at her. "You say this loss is your fault, right?"

"Yes," she whispered.

"Did you go to the drug store and buy over-the-counter next day emergency contraception?"

Her eyes widened. "Of course not!"

"Hmm. Did you provoke your husband so that he beat you about your tummy?"

Cathy sat, wincing. "David would never lift a hand to me!"

"Did you over-dose your birth control?"

"No!"

"Then why do you blame yourself?"

"My sins have found me out," she murmured.

"Pardon me?" Dr. Reynolds leaned closer.

She repeated, "My sins have found me out."

"What sins?"

"I am—"

"Was," David corrected.

"A prostitute. God is punishing me."

"Of course, like He punished Tamar and Rahab—two prostitutes in the lineage of Jesus? Or the woman at the well and the woman with an alabaster jar of oil?" Cathy stared at him as he continued, ". . . be not deceived: neither fornicators, nor idolaters, nor adulterers, nor effeminate, nor abusers of themselves with mankind, nor thieves, nor covetous, nor drunkards, nor revilers, nor extortioners, shall inherit the kingdom of God." Dr. Reynolds paused and took Cathy's hand. "And such **were** some of you: but ye are washed, but ye are sanctified, but you are justified in the name of the Lord Jesus, and by the Spirit of our God."

As David watched, a film that had darkened Cathy's countenance lifted.

Dr. Reynolds smiled gently. "Cathy, would you crucify our Lord again?" She shook her head. "Physically, I can release you today, but perhaps you should stay here one more day." He looked over at David. "Has John been here yet?"

"He's on his way."

The doctor paused, and Stanley pushed the door open. "Are you coming home today, Mama? Grandma said you might. I brought you clothes."

"It's up to the doctor. Dr. Reynolds, this is our son, Stanley."

Stanley grabbed his hand, almost knocking the clipboard out of it. "Please? Please, sir, can Mama come home? I'll be very good. I'll bring her tea. And Grandma will take care of Audrey Anne."

The doctor smiled at the boy, and rested his hand on his fair curls, so like hers. "You miss your mama, do you?"

The boy bobbed his head.

"Let's see what John says. If he concurs, I'll leave orders to dismiss her this afternoon." He looked at Stanley with mock severity. "Of course, if you don't take good care of Mama, we'll have to bring her back."

"Oh, we will, sir. I promise. Cross my heart."

He chuckled. "I believe you, Stanley." He winked at David. "I'll see her in two weeks and after that you two should be good to go—with protection. Let's wait another couple of months before you try for another baby." He waved and let himself out the door.

"Where is your grandmother?" David wanted to know.

"She's home with Audrey. Grandpa Clyde brought me. He's out there." Stanley waved in the direction of the waiting room.

David was relieved when the counselor from Hope House let himself in. Cathy raised her arms, and he gathered her close. David knew she loved this small, gentle man.

"I hear you've been in the Refiner's fire, Cathy. Are you rejoicing in the trying of your faith?"

"She didn't get burned, sir. We lost our baby, but he's with Jesus and we'll see him when we get to heaven," Stanley informed the stranger.

"This can't be Stanley? This young man with excellent theology?"

Stanley looked confused. "Do you know me?"

"I knew you when you were in Mama's tummy, and you've grown up to be a fine boy."

"Thank you, sir. Do you know my daddy? This is Dr. David Taylor." Stanley looked up proudly at David.

John shook David's hand. "I've met your dad several times, and I look forward to working with him."

Stanley tugged the small case over to David. "Grandpa Clyde said to leave this." He looked at John. "Excuse me, sir, I have to go. Bye, Mom, see ya later."

Cathy watched him open the door and go to find his grandfather.

"You look fine, Cathy. I heard a bad report."

"Dr. Reynolds corrected my stinking thinking. He quoted I Corinthians 6 to me. I realize what David's been saying is true. It wasn't my fault, but why, John?"

John pulled up a chair and sat. "That's a pretty easy one. You're getting ready to begin your ministry, and the enemy doesn't like challenges to his kingdom. You know the enemy, the one who comes to rob, kill, and destroy? The one who killed Job's children and stole his wealth?"

"Stanley said the other day, 'If Satan has any guts, I hate them, too,'" David told him.

John chuckled. "I like that kid! I hear he and Eddie are pretty thick."

They visited briefly, before John said, "Let's pray and get you out of here." After they prayed, he kissed Cathy on her forehead and went to the nurse's station.

When they arrived home, Stanley danced beside the car. He proudly opened the door and shoved a bunch of wildflowers into his mother's hand, but waited for David to help her out.

"Are you tired, Mama?"

"A little."

"I turned your bed down."

"Thank you. I love you."

"I love you, too, Mama, but Grandma says I shouldn't hug you too hard."

Grandma and Grandpa Clyde were holding the door open. Audrey Anne was waving her arms frantically and reaching for Cathy, but David took the little girl while Clyde gently escorted her mother to the downstairs bedroom.

"We made this up for you and David. Audrey and I will stay upstairs in your room until you can take the stairs," Clyde explained. "Are you hungry? You know your mother—she's cooked everything you like."

"Mostly tired right now. Maybe later."

"Of course, dear."

"Thank God He sent you, Clyde."

Clyde blinked hard several times, and his voice quavered as he replied, "Thank God He sent you, Miss Cathy."

Cathy figured out whenever Clyde called her that, he was remembering when she came to Stan, and she slipped her arm around his waist and leaned against him. Stanley ran ahead down the hall and was fluffing the pillows. She got in bed, and Clyde tucked the covers over her and asked if she needed anything. She reached up for Audrey, who wanted to snuggle in the worst way. David sat beside Cathy on the bed and tried to moderate the toddler's exuberance. The little one planted kisses all over her mother's face.

"Now, little miss, you've seen your mama. I told you she'd be here today. But that little kitty your Grandpa brought home for you needs some milk. Let's go feed her." Audrey held her hand out to the child, who came readily.

"We have a new family member?" Cathy asked.

"News to me," her husband replied. "But you can never have too many kitties when you live in the country." He dropped a gentle kiss on her lips. "You rest." He picked up a bell on the bedside table. "This must be Clyde's doing. Ring when you need service, Madame."

Later, Cathy wanted to eat at the table, so David walked her to the family dining area in the kitchen. She ate a few bites, mostly pushed food around the plate, and reached for a glass of milk. The drink shook ominously in her hand. Clyde, in a very butler-esque move, removed the glass from her hand and set it on the table.

"Perhaps you are ready to go back to bed?" he asked in a quiet voice.

She nodded, and he put his hand under her elbow. David tried not to hover and let Clyde walk her down the hall. Cathy paused and looked up at the tall thin man her mother had married, this grandfather her children loved. "I never knew what I missed until I saw David with his father. Clyde, would you be my father?"

Clyde gave a courteous little bow. "My dear, I've never been so honored. If you consent to be my daughter, I will be proud to be your father." Tears traced a track down his elegant face.

"May I hug you?"

He folded her in his arms, and they stood for a moment before he gently suggested they get her in bed.

Much later, after wrestling with Audrey Ann, and reading four stories with Stanley, David crawled into bed beside his wife. She instinctively curled into him, and his arms surrounded her. He brushed a kiss in her golden hair and breathed a quiet sigh. "I love you, Catherine Elizabeth Walker Taylor—more than words can say. I want you beside me every night of our lives. You are the best part of me. I was never a man until I knew you. God made you for me and brought you to me. You are His best gift."

Cathy's hand stole up to his face, and his tears rolled down his cheeks and over her hand, dripping into his tee shirt.

"Don't cry, David. I love you...'Thy people shall be my people, and thy God my God" where thou diest, I will die, and there will I be buried...' You are His best gift to me. Thank you for never letting go."

And they slept.

* * *

John, Beth, and Miss Ginny stopped by the next afternoon. While the ladies went to visit in the bedroom, John dropped down on a comfy chair on the deck across from David. Stanley had gone with his grandparents to look at the new construction, and Audrey was taking her nap, so David was reading his Bible. He looked up at John with a welcoming smile.

"Is she doing all right now? You were fortunate Dr. Reynolds was on call. Ben's a fine man," John said.

"As he spoke the Word, I saw a curtain of darkness rise, and light shone in her eyes."

"He sent His word and healed and delivered them."

"Amen."

"I'm always curious to follow up on our graduates. We hope they leave on their way to happiness, but relapses such as she had in the hospital do happen."

"We've been quite happy. It took me months to break down her defenses, but my mother was the one who set her free," and David told him about his brother, and then added his dad's advice. They had a good chuckle over that one.

"You were uniquely chosen for her, David."

"In many ways—Joe and I have gotten close, swapping war stories about loving abused women. Cathy's an amazing woman, John."

"Has she been able to be a good wife? —If you don't mind my asking."

"Candy was a huge help. They talked on the phone, and she told her the books you and Beth used when they were on this road. Cathy's very responsive and generous. She doesn't initiate, and her night clothes are conservative. I bought her something more...tempting...once, but I found it in the back of the closet, still in the bag."

"That's understandable. She doesn't want to remind you—or herself—of her past."

"I understand. It's easy for me. I didn't know her then, and she's a new creation—I can't even envision that time in her life. I have no complaints. Clyde has helped me to understand a lot. Stan Foster, Stanley's grandfather, adopted him and left him his estate. Clyde was Stan's butler."

"Audrey's husband?"

"Yes. He first met Cathy when she went to visit Stan on his death bed. Clyde absolutely adores Cathy and her mother. He told me when she came to Chicago to see Stan as he was dying, he thought she was a conniving female out to exploit the old man, but she genuinely loved him—he and the attorney, even the hospice nurse, saw it."

"She told me once Stan was the first man who ever loved her," John said.

"She told me that, too, and from what she's told me about her father, I believe it. Stan left her a fortune."

"I heard. How do you feel about that?"

David laughed. "Okay, once I got over myself— I struggled with my masculine pride—but Clyde filled me in on a lot of those details. Now, I accept it as God's provision. She and Allen, Stan's attorney, are setting up a charitable foundation. Allen said Stan set up a trust for Stanley because he figured she'd give it all away. She manages the fund and already has enough set aside for his college. Stan told Allen she's good through and through. She is. She's the most pure-hearted person I've ever known." David blinked his glistening eyes. "Her father must be a piece of work. Last night, she asked Clyde if he would be her father."

John leaned forward and dropped his head. The two men prayed for Cathy and for the paths of service before this couple.

"Why did you decide to move to Columbus?" John wanted to know.

David paused. "This is the closest to home Cathy has. Her life started here—Hope House, where she found Christ, her dearest friends, who are like sisters, have reunions here. I'm secure in my home and family. I grew up in a close family, four brothers, and parents who are still very much in love after forty-four years. I'm one of those folks who can't remember not having God in my life. Mom says I asked Jesus into my life when I was three. I don't know—coming here seemed like the right thing to do. And my wife bought me an orchard. I grew up in an orchard."

"In the book of Acts, I love the phrase 'it seemed good to us and the Holy Spirit.' Sometimes it's all you know to do—what seems good to you."

David stood and pointed to the trees. "Want to walk?" As they meandered, he said they'd been tossing around ideas about letting some of the Hope House girls who were able do seasonal labor, harvesting the fruit, making cider, and canning, maybe even manning a fruit stand.

"Being around the two of you would be good for them. Tom, Beth's husband, has served as a good role model for them through the years. My wife teaches at the college, so we haven't been able to be a couple living our lives in front of them as much, although we try to have them over to the house sometimes. I heard an old Mennonite man say one time, 'There's more caught than taught.' They need to see loving couples in committed relationships."

"Cathy opened up in my family. She thanks me for giving her a family, and they all love her. We prayed about moving near the orchard in Washington, but God drew us here, to Hope House."

"Daddy." Stanley's cry turned their steps back to the house. He was eager to tell David about the earth movers, and tomorrow the cement trucks would be there, and Grandpa promised he could go see. "Could Eddie come over? His uncle is building the house, you know."

"Let's ask Mommy if he can spend the night. Don't you have soccer tonight?"

"Yes, sir."

"If it's all right with Mom and Aunt Candy, we can bring him back here after practice so you can be there early in the morning. Of course, you'll have to go to sleep tonight."

"I will, Daddy. I promise." The boy slipped his hand in David's. "Grandma has lunch ready. Will you stay with us, Mr. John?"

"I believe that's the plan," he affirmed.

* * *

Cathy was up and about in three days, but David suggested she remain home until after she saw Dr. Reynolds. Although she was a bit weepy, she recovered her strength. She came by the office a couple of times to supervise the placement of her desk and file cabinets. They selected a conference table and chairs for the conference room. She loved the light green drapes and wanted to shop for some area rugs. The place was shaping up nicely, and David was already seeing clients referred to him by John and Dr. Ben Reynolds. David had visited several pastors around town to talk to them and present his credentials. Often pastors were too busy to do in-depth counseling, but they wanted to ensure their congregants were receiving Christian services. He recognized they would find a place of service in Columbus. Cathy suggested they host an Open House, and she began gathering names and addresses to send out invitations. She called caterers and selected a menu. Carlos Rodriguez was on the Chamber of Commerce, was a well-respected businessman in the area, and his influence drew in many potential clients.

David also discovered she was planning a Hope House event at their home. He caught her on the phone as he came into the house. "I see you're not working again. He grinned and leaned down for a kiss. "What time is your appointment tomorrow?"

"Ten. Mom and Clyde are watching the kids—wanna go out to lunch after?"

Giving her a meaningful look, he replied, "Do you really want to know what I want to do after? Maybe check into a hotel. How would you like that?" And he took her into his arms and kissed her like he hadn't kissed her in two weeks.

"That'd be good," she said into his lips, and then she swatted his behind. He laughed and asked what event she was planning at the house Friday evening. She explained she was inviting Hope House staff and supporters—donors and volunteers from their church and the Catholic churches.

"About twenty or so?" he asked.

"More like a hundred. I've ordered a tent for the yard in case it rains. Candy and I are going to call Missy O'Malley about a fundraiser in the fall. She sings beautifully. She sang us through our labor and delivery. Who do you think should speak?"

"Hope House girls, past and present—we overcome by the Blood of the Lamb and the Word of our testimony—and you don't have to pay them."

Of the three upcoming events, David most looked forward to the return to the garden of his delights, as his father referred to the marriage bed. He wasn't disappointed, but Cathy struggled with the protection the doctor insisted they use. David reminded her they had conceived two children on her birth control pill. She hated using protection and told him Donnie required "his girls" use protection every time, and he also screened them for STDs monthly. She shuddered.

David held her for a time, speaking words of love and stroking her until his slow caresses and deep kisses awakened her and she was more than ready.

The following night he came out of the shower, towel-drying his hair. Cathy had the sheet over her, up to her neck, and he asked if she wanted him to turn down the AC.

"No, I want you to get in bed."

When he got under the covers, he discovered she was naked. That was a first! He quickly joined her, throwing his pajamas on the floor, and made it worth her while. The garden of his delights was growing.

The Open House Thursday afternoon was a huge success. From 3-7 p.m. guests filtered through their offices. Candy's sister-in-law, Merida a graphic designer, had created lovely brochures and cards for each of them. Their supply was well depleted when everyone left, and Cathy sank into a chair. The caterers came to carry off their settings and noted not much food was left over for tomorrow's Friday night event.

"Those were for appetizers anyway. We're having ribs, corn, and salads for dinner," Cathy said, but she agreed to order more. David noted she wasn't using the business checkbook, and she said this wasn't like the Open House; it was for Hope House.

"Be sure you note that on the check, so you can take a charitable deduction," David suggested. "I know these are your friends, but it's a Hope House outreach, right? Stan was a smart businessman—I'm sure he wants you to be prudent."

Cathy walked away from her desk and went over to him to lean her head on his chest. "Thank you," she whispered. She returned to her desk and finished writing out the check and then sent the caterers away.

"What was that for?"

"The hug?"

"Yeah."

"Because..." Tears seeped from her eyes. Once again David wondered how long they would, and what he had done this time. "I...it means a lot to me that you...think of Stan kindly. He was good to me."

David drew her into his arms and rested his chin on her head. "I know. He was the first man who ever loved you." She nodded against his chest. "But now you have quite a collection: me, my dad, my brothers, and Clyde— plus John."

"I know," she sniffed. "I'm blessed."

"You, my Love, are a blessing."

* * *

Friday night Beth asked if she and Tom could come by early, and she invited Candy and Joe to be there as well. She had something to ask them, she said. Cathy had a tray of iced tea on the deck—next year it would be their cider.

"What's the mystery, Beth?" Cathy asked.

"You two have been great supporters of Hope House, but I need a different kind of help." Tom dropped his hand on her shoulder, grinning with pride. "You see, at the ripe old age of 46, I'm pregnant again. We've made if through the first trimester, so it's happening."

Joe and David high-fived Tom, congratulating him on nailing another one!

"Only this egg is an old one, making this a high-risk pregnancy. We've refused amino, of course, because we'll take whatever God gives us, but I'm required to rest, and that means time off. I was hoping, Cathy, before your practice gets too full, that you would cover for me for the next year or so. Would you consider that? Pray about it?"

"No need to pray—it's an opportunity to pay it forward. I can never repay Hope House for what you've meant to me. It will be an honor and a privilege, won't it, David?" He agreed, with a smile, knowing how happy this would make his wife.

"Another thing before you decide. We're announcing Miss Ginny's retirement tonight. The Board has hired her replacement."

Cathy's head swiveled to Candy. She was on the Board and hadn't breathed a word.

"We're very pleased, Cathy," Candy said. "Gayle Wilson has been working with the youth at our church for several years and helping out at Hope House. Ginny's been working with her. You'll love her!"

"I saw her name on the list, but I couldn't remember her."

"Her husband died three years ago. They moved here after you left. I put her at our table."

The doorbell began to ring then and Clyde assumed his post, welcoming everyone inside the house. Appetizers were served on the deck, and dinner was served inside the white tent in the yard. A trio of musicians played soft music in the background. Cathy did feel comfortable with Gayle and knew they would work together well. Beth needed Cathy right away, so the next week she began to work three mornings a week; because Hope House was a part time job, she could pick up a few clients at the office. Their accountant advised them to pay Clyde and Audrey for childcare because they could take daycare off their taxes. Although they protested, Cathy and David insisted. They dropped the kids off in the mornings throughout the rest of the summer; in the fall, Clyde met Stanley's school bus at the end of the lane.

Life settled into a comfortable routine. Cathy and Gayle prayed over their girls, and Cathy helped each one to make a plan for her baby. The group was all teenagers who had been careless; some boyfriends were helpful, most were not; but, everyone who placed for adoption had to have both parents sign the surrender. They planned a fundraising dinner at Thanksgiving because the time worked out for Missy. She worked at Lowe's in Elkins and had to accrue enough vacation time, since she'd only recently moved from her first interior decorating job at Penney's in Clarksburg.

Stanley and David looked forward to meeting this nearly mythological creature—the girl Candy and Cathy loved—and when she arrived and they found a petite brown-skinned, black-haired pixie tugging her suitcase out of her car. "Here, let me get that," David said, taking it out of her hand. "I'm David."

"Of course, you're David, and this—this fine young man—can't possibly be Stanley? You look like you're 12 years old!"

Stanley was used to his mother's friends knowing him, but he shifted from one foot to the other nevertheless, blushing. He didn't know whether to extend his hand or expect an embrace, but his mother solved his dilemma by rushing out of the house, screaming, and hugging the newcomer.

Cathy drew Stanley to her side. "You've heard Mommy and Aunt Candy talk about Aunt Missy, remember?"

He shyly reached out to shake her hand. "My sister's in the house. You want to meet her? She's walking now."

They followed David into the house, with Missy jabbing her friend with her elbow and protesting she hadn't told her how handsome her husband was. David shook his head, winked at Stanley, and led them upstairs to the bedroom where Missy would be staying.

Missy asked Stanley if he knew his mother and she had roomed together years ago at Hope House. She wanted to see the kitten, now a sleek, silver cat. Stanly watched, astounded, as she crossed her legs and folded them under her, sitting and extending her hands to hold him. Then she walked in the orchard with Stanley, talking to him like he was one of the grown-ups. She listened seriously, asked questions, and soon had him chattering away like they were old friends. He liked this Aunt Missy!

"How did you do that?" he asked.

"What?"

"That sitting-down thing."

"Ah, you know I'm an Indian maid, right? It's an old trick of ours." She showed him how to take a small step back, bend his knee and bring the other leg in front. He tumbled over the first time he tired, but she laughingly pulled him up several times until he could do it, too. He was fascinated to learn she was an Indian! She brought Mom a papoose board so they could take walks with Audrey Anne.

Eddie and Stanley hung around on the deck. Candy and her family arrived after she closed the shop. Little Rod, a few months younger than Audrey, was pulling up. The parents sat around the family room while the babies played together. David and Joe wandered out to the deck to put meat on the grill—hamburgers for the boys, steaks for the adults. They agreed the Hope House girls shared a special bond. David grilled veggies and baked potatoes. Cathy brought a big tossed salad and set it on the table before scooting under David's arm.

"How's it coming?" He dropped a kiss on her nose and asked for a platter and a fork. He took off the steaks at the requested times of medium-rare to well-done; they sat in the evening light and ate on the deck. Stanley and Eddie learned a lot about their mothers that night! Aunt Missy promised to teach them how to short sheet a bed. And they laughed. Stanley had never seen his mother laugh so much, and Daddy shook his head and smiled the special smile he had for her—the one that made Stanley feel so warm inside. Aunt Candy and Mommy went inside to put the babies down, and the boys were delighted the Longs were spending the night. They talked late, but they still heard the adults downstairs when they finally drifted off.

The next day, the women closeted themselves away to plan for the evening banquet. Grandma and Grandpa wanted to go to the dinner, so one of Uncle Carlos' girls would stay with the boys—Stanley thought it was Consuela, but he couldn't keep the big Rodriguez family straight yet. At least they wouldn't have to sit through boring old speeches! But when they heard Aunt Missy practicing, they kind of wanted to hear her sing. Mommy said she'd sing in church Sunday, and he didn't have to go to children's church.

Saturday morning, Joe went to work, and Daddy sat at his desk to study while the boys played. That afternoon, mommies dressed up really pretty and the daddies put on suits. After the dinner, the house was filled with the Rodriguez family. Stanley and Eddie laughed at how loud they were and hoped they wouldn't wake the babies. Consuela did good getting them to sleep! Eddie's grandmother, Martha, was always quiet, but she never fussed when they all talked at once. She was like Stanley's grandma somehow. Quiet, but nice and patient-like. Eddie's grandfather, who was called Rod by most people but Mario by Martha, hovered around her the way Clyde did Stanley's grandmother. From what the boys understood, the banquet was a huge success. They had to bring in extra tables, and they raised lots of money—and their mommies and Aunt Missy made the speeches! Stanley decided living around Columbus was lots of fun.

Stanley couldn't believe it the next morning when Daddy woke him for church. It was too late for Sunday school. He and Eddie scrambled into their church clothes. They wanted to hear Aunt Missy sang, and they agreed it was like listening to an angel! When Daddy put her suitcase into her car, Stanley wasn't shy at all. He threw his arms around her and begged her to come back. She ruffled his hair and told him he and his family had to come to the mountains of West Virginia and see her. She had a nephew, she told him, who had red hair. The mommies hugged and cried and prayed for safe travel, and she pulled off with a wave. Stanley sighed. Everyone left, and it was only Mommy and Daddy and Audrey Anne. They watched a Pixar film and Mommy made popcorn. Stanley felt Daddy carry him upstairs, and then he helped, him put on his pajamas. He heard Mommy come up the stairs and Daddy laughing and whispering to her as they went down the hall.

Sister-Mother

Cathy picked up her phone at the office and heard the anxiety in Gayle's voice. "Cathy, Kentucky Human Services dropped our new girl off a day early. She's not happy and vows she's going to run away. Is there any way you can see her today?"

Cathy glanced up at the clock and shifted her computer to her schedule. "Let me make a few calls and I'll be right there." She canceled a planning meeting, rearranged a few appointments, told David where she would be, and left for Hope House. She caught Gayle in the kitchen, and she pointed upstairs. "She's locked herself in. The other girls have gone to school or jobs, but she wouldn't even eat breakfast with us. Middle bedroom. God help you."

The substitute social worker swallowed hard as she mounted the stairs. *God, I need you. You know this girl–please, help me to reach her. Give me Your love for her.*

She knocked at the door of the room she shared with Missy several years ago. "Mary Rose, it's Cathy, the social worker. I came to see how I can help you."

To Cathy's surprise, the door banged open. Cathy glanced around the newly painted but still light-yellow room. One bed was neatly made, the other rumpled and tossed. Remembering her time with Missy, the laughter and the tears, she smiled. "This was my room once–I lived with a girl named Missy O'Malley. I hope you and Suzette will become as close friends as we did."

"I'm not staying! I can't stay; my brother and sisters need me, but the state won't let me be with them because I'm pregnant. I want to get rid of this baby and take care of them again, but they say I'm too young. I'm going to steal them if I have to. I'm all they've got."

"Wow, I see where you're coming from, and your devotion to your family is terrific. Let's see what we can do about it. Get dressed and come down to the office, so you can tell me all about it."

A flicker of hope crossed the thin face. Mary Rose pushed her stringy bleached hair off her face and glared at Cathy. "You lying to me?"

"Mary Rose, one thing you need to learn at Hope House is that we are on your side. We'll do everything in our power for you, but I need to know what's going on. Will you come downstairs and talk to me?"

She nodded her head, but wariness remained in her eyes. "Lemme get dressed."

"Do you know where my office is?"

"I'll meet you at the foot of the stairs."

"Have you eaten?"

"No."

"I'll get you some food and meet you in ten."

"Okay."

Gayle looked up as Cathy walked into the kitchen. When she explained the plan, Gayle suggested they eat in the yard since it was a beautiful day. But Cathy wanted Mary Rose to see the fetal models and baby pictures, since she indicated termination, so the two ladies wrestled a tray table into the office.

The office was right beside the stairs, so Cathy heard the girl and met her. Seeing her in her blue jeans without the bulky shirt, Cathy realized she already showed—she was far along to have an abortion. The girl eyed the breakfast hungrily, and Cathy waved her in.

"Gayle and I brought a tray table in for you." She stepped back and the teenager edged forward, frightened as a stray puppy. Cathy longed to put her arms around her, but she sensed the girl would bolt, so she smiled instead and asked if she liked scrambled eggs. Mary Rose sat, picked up her fork and plunged in, stuffing her mouth with eggs and toast, and swallowing a gulp of orange juice to wash it all down. The girl was hungry.

"When did you eat last? I'll have to take this up with Miss Gayle if she's not feeding your girls properly!"

Mary Rose glared at Cathy. "She fixed ham and macaroni and cheese last night, but I wasn't hungry. Leastways, I didn't want to eat. I couldn't eat. I have to talk to the kids."

"I'll see if we can't arrange that today."

"You'd help me talk to them?"

"You won't relax until you do."

"I'm all they've got. They must think I've run off on them, too."

"Who else ran off on them?"

"My mom left last summer—about July. Social Services came and took them away while I was...working, making money. They wouldn't let me see them or talk to them. I had to take care of them. I know it was that old busybody next door who called and said Benny was crying."

"Tell me about your family," Cathy said, pulling her chair beside the girl and leaning forward.

She learned about Tessa, ten, Maude, seven, and Benny, four. Their mother had left last July, and Mary Rose had been looking after them ever since. They lived in a rented trailer in Kentucky, near Lexington. Cathy found out she paid her rent by giving sex to the landlord, and pulled out the rest of the story: she paid utilities and bought food by selling her body. But she and the children went to school every day. She got birth control from the school health clinic, but apparently slipped up and got pregnant several months ago.

"You think I'm a bad person, Miss Cathy, but it was the only way. I knew if the welfare found out, they'd separate us, just like they did. They sent me up here and said I couldn't have any contact with them. I was unfit. The kids are somewhere in Kentucky—I've got to talk to them!"

"You're a remarkable person, Mary Rose, and your sisters and brother are blessed to have you. I'm going to make every effort to see if we can't get a phone call made today." Cathy picked up her file. "I'll have to do a little research. Do you want to stay with me while I make some calls?" Knowing decisions had been made without her input and realizing how out of control the girl felt, Cathy let her sit and listen while she tracked down the children's social worker. She was quiet but firm, insisting she had to speak with her today. Then she let her hear the explanation of why this older sister needed to speak with her siblings. She even heard her defend her—she sounded angry. How else was she to provide for them? Didn't she get them to school? Were their clothes clean? Was the house clean?

Mary Rose heard Cathy say many nice things about herself. Then she gave her a thumbs-up and a triumphant grin saying, "I'll sit with her and make sure that doesn't happen, Ms. Fisher, but it is imperative for her own psychological health that she knows they are fine. And, I submit to you the children will settle in and behave better when they have talked to her as well. In fact, if we schedule some regular calls and they go well, perhaps I can bring her down for a visit. No, no promises, we'll talk about that later. Yes, thank you so much."

Cathy fought tears.

"Wow," Mary Rose said. "You stuck up for me. Why are you so emotional about my problems? Are those pictures of your husband and kids in the frame on your desk? Your life is good, why did you care about a strange kid from Kentucky, one who sold her body?"

Cathy beamed. "I'll get to that later. Here's the deal. I've got the phone number—they're all at the same foster home, kind of a miracle itself. That's good because they've had one another. I'm to monitor the call; that means I sit beside you and make sure you don't say anything bad about their foster home or make any promises we can't keep. If the call goes well—if the kids don't behave badly after their phone visits—and you truly help them, maybe we can work out a visit later. How does that sound?"

Mary Rose was fighting tears. Cathy moved back in front of the table, and this time, she took her in her arms. The girl let fall the tears she had held back, and sobbed her thanks.

"It seems they're doing okay. They're in school, and Ms. Fisher is going to tell the foster mother to allow your call to go through. What you need to do is support and encourage them, tell them you love them and if they are good, maybe we'll arrange a visit."

"How can I get to Kentucky?"

"Mary Rose, I'll take you myself."

"Why would you do that for me?"

"You are a very brave girl. You've cared for those kids, and I bet they love you very much—as much as you love them."

"But..."

"No buts, except but what can we do for you? Let's talk about you and that baby you are carrying. Let's think about you; let's put you first. Can you handle that?"

"I can't handle a baby, God knows. It's all I can do to take care of the three I have."

Cathy talked to the frightened girl about abortion, the risks and dangers of the procedure itself as well as the stage of her baby. She showed her the fetal models, estimating the size of her baby. The teenager stroked the soft rubber models. Cathy asked if she felt movement, and the girl wasn't sure. They'd check on a doctor's appointment.

"You don't have to make decisions right away. We need to gather the facts. We have wonderful Christian homes who long for a baby. You can place your baby, knowing he or she will be loved and cared for."

"That's not wrong—to give away your baby?"

"No, Mary Rose, sometimes it's the most loving thing a mother can do. My roommate placed her baby."

"But you—you didn't?"

"No, I didn't." Cathy picked up the framed picture and pointed Stanley out. "Stanley is eight now. And this is my husband and Stanley's sister, Audrey Anne."

"Gosh, he looks nice."

Cathy smiled. "He is, very, and you'll get to know them all. We'd like you to come out to our place soon, with all the other girls."

"I can't figure you out."

Cathy chuckled. "When I came to Hope House, I found a lot of wonderful people who helped me build a new life."

"Why didn't you give your baby away?"

"That's a long story, and everyone's different. We each make our own choices—but I had a wonderful mother who helped me. I went to college, where I met my husband. God has given Stanley the best father in the world.

Now, first things first. Let's talk to Miss Gayle about a doctor's appointment for you."

Tucking Mary Rose's arm under her own, Cathy led her to the kitchen. Gayle wasn't there, but they spotted her sitting in the garden. They pushed open the door and asked if they could join her. She was planning to go inside and fix a snack for the girls coming home from summer school. She told Cathy the appointment was scheduled for two days from then—a day after Mary Rose's expected arrival.

She ducked her head. "They brought me early because I threatened to run away and they wanted to get me out of state. But I would have made my way back to the kids."

"And now?" Gayle asked.

"Miss Cathy made arrangements for me to talk to them today, after school. And maybe even visit later. She said if the calls go well and the kids are okay, maybe we can go see them; and it's not so bad here, I guess." She looked at Gayle with remorse. "Thank you for breakfast, and I'm sorry I was mean."

"You were worried about your brother and sisters. I get that."

"Let's go inside and help get this snack ready," Cathy suggested. "I have to stick around until after this phone call."

"I won't upset them. I promise. I want to tell them I love them and hear that they're okay."

"You need to give them permission to be okay. They might feel like they're betraying you to like their foster home."

"Like I felt about coming here? I felt bad because everyone was so nice to me and doing for me when I felt like I'd run off on them and let them down."

"How old are you, Mary Rose?" Cathy asked.

"Fourteen."

The social worker leaded over and covered her hand with her own. "It's okay to be a kid at fourteen. Let us help you—so you can better help them, deal?"

Mary Rose blinked, swiped her eyes, and bobbed her head. "Deal."

165

"I promise we won't take them away, and we'll try our very best to get you back together as a family."

Mary Rose sat close to Cathy as the girls piled in, talking about their adventures at school. Two of the older girls were working this summer. Cathy realized the newcomer was the youngest girl in the house, but certainly not the least responsible. For almost a year, she had been more of a mother than a sister to three little ones.

The phone call was made, and Cathy listened to the excited voices on the other end of the line. She tried to fool with papers, but she listened to Mary Rose instruct her siblings to be good, to be obedient and do their homework, not to listen to too much TV, and she encouraged Tess to read to the little ones. At the end of the conversation, she reminded them that they had to be very good, so she could call again. "No more flushing things down the toilet, Benny. You go apologize to Mrs. Duggan when we hang up, okay?" She made kissing sounds and asked if they caught them before she put the phone down and cried.

"They're okay, Cathy. Thank you. They don't have any books though— can we send them some books?"

"I'll get the address, and we'll send them some books. Did you read to them?"

"Yes, Ma'am. I was saving to get computer stuff, baby Einstein stuff, but I read on the computer they shouldn't have more than an hour a day. I didn't have a computer, but I looked it up in the school library. Made me feel better, 'cause I couldn't buy all that electronic stuff, and I could check books out of the library for free. They're really smart for their age. They make A's and B's."

"You've done a fine job with them."

"You should see the notes I got from school about how they'd shown 'significant improvement.' I was mad when mom left us, but we've all done better since she left."

Mary Rose was surprised when Cathy pulled her to herself and kissed her gently on the cheek before she left.

As she walked through the kitchen, Gayle said thanks quietly. Overcome with emotion, Cathy waved and left.

As she drove to the office, her cell phone rang. Conveniently near a parking lot, she pulled in, surprised to hear Mrs. Duggan telling her how wonderful the call had been, how good for the children, and laughing about Benny apologizing for his pranks. She urged her to let their sister call them anytime.

When she got to the office, David wasn't behind his desk. He sat in a big chair, but he had several files on his lap, and his hand rested on them. She could tell he was praying for his patients. She moved to stand in front of him. He lifted the charts to his desk and opened his arms. She slipped into his lap and wept. He held her, resting his chin on her head.

"Tough?"

Lifting her tear-streaked face, Cathy told him about a fourteen-year old child who mothered three younger siblings and sold her body to support them.

"You know what I thought, David?" He waited. "This poor child was called unfit, but she didn't know any other way to support her brother and sisters. I was making money for a pimp and saving the rest for college, covering my tracks because I ran away. She was feeding and taking care of three kids!"

He lowered his head and brushed her lips. "God brought her the perfect social worker. You can share the righteousness God has given with her."

"She's so much more worthy!"

He shook his head and swatted her bottom. "None of us are righteous, Mrs. Taylor. Only God is righteous."

"But I am His child, and I've inherited it from Him."

"You're finally getting it. Let's go get our kids. Did you tell her about yourself?"

"Not yet, but I will—I must. I'm a debtor."

A Trip with Mary Rose

D avid loaded the suitcases in the car and turned to Cathy. "Ready?"
"I can't believe you and Audrey are going with me."

"We'll make a mini-vacation out of it."

They stopped by Hope House and picked up the fourteen- year old, now obviously pregnant. She scooted in beside Audrey's car seat and looked around for Stanley. When she asked where he was, Cathy told her he was spending the weekend with a friend. "Eddie is a Hope House baby, too. His mom lived there when I did."

"Is she married now?"

"She is. She married Joe in Hope House, and he adopted Eddie. They have another son a little younger than Audrey Anne." Noting the girl's quizzical look, she added, "There is life after Hope House, Mary Rose."

David looked in the rear-view mirror. "Did you like pastor's sermon Sunday from Jeremiah? God has a plan for us, and a future. He is a merciful God, and delivers us from our destructions."

"Thanks for doing this, Mr. David."

"My pleasure, sweetie." He winked at her, but it wasn't the ugly leering winks she was used to. It was open and friendly, and made her feel warm inside. "Give her the Amazon box, Cath."

Cathy lifted it over the seat, and Mary Rose leafed through Nancy Drew mysteries and an abridged *Little Women.* "David is one of a slew of boys, so he had to do some research on girls' books—lots of the new ones are not godly, but these are old reliables. He figured Benny would like them, too, if Tessa read them to him. They chatted and drove. Poor Mary Rose was stuck entertaining Audrey, but she played with her and read her little story books until the little girl fell asleep.

"She can get a rest before we get there. It's only about three hours to Lexington and Nicholasville is about 35 miles south," David told Mary Rose. "We should be there by 3:30, when your sisters and brother get home from school."

Mary Rose bounced in her seat. Cathy reached back and squeezed her hand. "I like your hair. Did Miss Gayle take you to Candy?"

"Yes, Ma'am. Do you know her?"

"She's Eddie's mom, where Stanley is staying tonight."

"Oh, she's the one who was there with you?"

"Yep. She serves on the Board now. We owe Hope House."

"Aren't they coming to the barbecue next week?" David asked.

"They are. You'll meet them then."

"Cathy made wonderful friends at Hope House, lifelong friends. You should see one of the reunions—I've never heard so much excitement and female squeals in my life."

Mary Rose giggled. "I like my new friends, too. I hope we'll stay friends. You sure get to know someone quick when you share your troubles."

David had programmed the foster home into his GPS, so he pulled up in front of it. The yellow school bus stopped down the street. He pointed and winked at Cathy. "Good timing, wouldn't you say?"

"Oh, is that their bus, you reckon?" Mary Rose tugged frantically at the door handle and all but fell out of the car. She stood beside it, scanning the kids getting off the bus. "Tessa! Maudie, Ben." Three kids lifted their heads at the sound and ran, full tilt, into her outstretched arms. They knocked her over, and she plopped on the ground. They leapt over and around her, tugging her up into hugs.

Ben jumped into her arms, and she snuggled into his neck. Tessa softly touched her hair. "I like your hair, Mary Rose. It looks so soft and pretty."

Maude clung to her leg, chanting, "You came, you came."

David wrapped his arms around his wife. "You made all this joy happen, sweetheart."

"God gave me favor with the social worker. They weren't going to let her see them again because she was—"

"You told me. Look at that! Have you ever seen such love?"

"Yeah, at Taylor Farms. Isn't she great, David?" Cathy's eyes shone with love and pride for her charge. Looking up she saw a plump, grey-haired lady approaching them with a huge smile, and she knew her before she opened her mouth. "Mrs. Duggan, how can we ever thank you for letting us come? Mary Rose has hardly slept for two days!"

"Those three have been beside themselves. Let's go inside." She raised her voice. "Who wants lemonade and cookies?"

Herding a chorus of "I do's," she led them into her simple home. David told Cathy to go ahead, he'd bring Audrey. He picked up the toddler, who was no longer sleeping but standing up in his arms to see all the excitement. He tended to the first order of business, getting her to the bathroom, and joined the family at the kitchen table. Mrs. Duggan's home was a simple house, kid-friendly, with soccer balls, kick balls and basketballs stacked in a big plastic bin in the corner. Everyone seemed to talk at once, and Mary Rose kept up. She looked at the kids' grade cards that had been set out for her visit and praised their school work. They tugged her by her hand to their room.

"I tried to put Benny in a room of his own, since he's a boy, but he cried so hard for her, Mr. Duggan said we should put them together—don't tell Ms. Fisher."

"Ms. Fisher is the state social worker," Cathy informed her husband.

"Mum's the word."

"I have a room for him, and his things are mostly in there, but he was so heart-broken. She's tough. How did you get her to agree to let Mary Rose call? If I'd known where to call, I would have. She took such good care of those kids!"

"God gave me favor, Mrs. Duggan."

"Please call me Clara."

"Sure, Clara, and I'm Cathy, and this is my husband, David."

"And Audrey. I heard." Clara Duggan ruffled the tot's curls. "She's all you, Cathy." Clara said God must have intervened, because Ms. Fisher had said Mary Rose couldn't ever be reunited with the children because she . . ..

"I know. She told me, Clara. She did what she could, the only way she knew how. She had no other means to support them."

"I guess boys lined up outside the trailer. She would go to their cars, but one night one of them drove off with her, and Benny woke up. The neighbor called the police and by the time he brought her home, the police were waiting and took her to juvie." Mrs. Duggan wiped her eyes. "Clean as a whistle, they were, and crying for her all the time. They let me go back to the trailer so the kids could get their clothes. It was squeaky clean, and all the clothes put neatly in drawers and closets. I don't know how a child so young could do that. The place was spotless."

"She said she wanted to cover any traces of the fact that a grown-up wasn't there," Cathy said.

"I told that Ms. Fisher she took care of those kids good as anybody, but she said she was a prostitute. Mary Rose did good with them—it was 'yes, ma'am' and 'no, sir" and they did their chores. I never had to pick up a towel, and they made their beds, too. They said Mary Rose told them they had to help each other out so they could stay together."

"May I take you and your husband with us to dinner?" David asked.

"He'll be working late. He's the school janitor, and they're having a dance tonight—but it gets us overtime."

"Then you join us—what do you suggest?"

"The kids all love Denny's."

"Denny's it is then."

"Go see Rosie," Audrey insisted, scrambling off her father's lap and looking around the corner.

*   *   *

"I'll take you, poppet," Clara Duggan said, holding out her hand. Audrey looked back to her mother, who joined them to walk down the hall. In the children's room, a double bed and a single bed filled the space. The white chenille spreads were worn, but clean, and the room was tidy. White curtains fluttered in the breeze coming through the open window, but the kids weren't in there. They were in the next room, because they had more play space in a room with only a twin bed. All the books Mary Rose had sent were lined up in a bookshelf Sam Duggan had made, that was put up above the dresser. The spread in this, the boy's room, was brown and orange plaid.

Maude and Benny stopped tumbling over Mary Rose to consider the little girl.

Tessa held out her hand and invited her to join them. "Maybe, if we can be *quiet*, Mary Rose will read to us."

"We played *I Spy* in the car," Mary Rose told them. "I spy something green." And the guesses and laughter began.

Clara and Cathy heard David calling for them, and they found him with Ms. Fisher in the living room. She had come by to meet Mary Rose and see if the visit was a good thing.

"Listen to them! They are so happy to see their sister," Mrs. Duggan said.

"Dr. Taylor said he is impressed with Mary Rose. His wife is the social worker at Hope House. They are both licensed counselors." Ms. Fisher was impressed with the credentials David had given. "And you are Ms. Taylor?" Ms. Fisher extended her hand to Cathy.

"Cathy, Cathy Taylor. David and I both got our degrees at Wheaton University, near Chicago. We met there. He was the graduate student teacher in one of my courses."

David grinned. "My wife threatened to sue me for sexual harassment."

"I did not!"

"Sounded like it to me," he teased. "I had to court her son to get anywhere near her."

"You had a child, Ms. Taylor?"

"I was a Hope House girl myself, Ms. Fisher. That's how I know lives can be changed and redirected. Hope House enabled me to get a GED, and I went to the community college in Columbus for two years before transferring to Wheaton."

"Oh. So, you are working with Mary Rose?"

"Right now, she plans to give the baby up for adoption—do you have any information about who the father might be?"

"There were...so many. I couldn't even guess. I couldn't find a place for her, with her history. I hope she isn't contagious."

"We've had her tested. She has no STD's," Cathy said. David put his arm around his wife's stiffening back.

"That's a relief." Ms. Fisher turned to Mrs. Duggan. "She's in there? With the children? May I see her?"

"You should have seen those kids running up the street when they saw her. They haven't let her go yet." Mrs. Duggan led the social worker down the hall, and Cathy followed.

Audrey was on Mary Rose's lap and her brother and sisters were leaning against her, listening to her read. The younger children scrambled up. "Mary Rose," Tessa said, "this is Ms. Fisher, the social worker from the state. This is my big sister."

"Who is this little one?"

Mary Rose stood, her hand on Audrey's shoulder. "This is Dr. and Mrs. Taylor's daughter, Audrey Anne."

"Well, Mary Rose, you have a nice weekend and don't upset the children."

Biting her tongue, the teenager murmured, "Yes, ma'am. Thank you for allowing me to visit. Mrs. Duggan is very nice."

"Yes, this is a good placement, and we don't want to see it disrupted."

"No, ma'am."

"Very well, then." Ms. Fisher turned and went down the hall. When she was safely out of sight, Maudie stuck her tongue out.

Giggling, Tessa and Mary Rose told her not to do that, but Cathy had a hard time suppressing her own giggle.

"We have to keep secrets from her. She won't let Benny sleep with us," Tessa said adding, "We didn't know what to say when she asked why Uncle Sam put the double bed in our room and moved the twin in here. I said I was a restless sleeper," Tessa added.

"Where's Daddy?" Audrey Anne asked.

"Come on, we'll take you to him," Mary Rose said. Entering the living room, she peered around. "Is she gone yet?" she whispered.

"Yes, after finding out you would stay at the hotel with Dr. and Mrs. Taylor. That's my story, and I'm sticking to it," Mrs. Duggan said, "but we do have an unused bed…"

David put his arm around Mrs. Duggan. "You, Clara, are a woman after my own heart." He turned to the little ones, dropping on one knee to be eye level with Benny. "Aunt Clara says you like Denny's." The boy's face lit up and he bobbed his head. "Go wash up then, so we can beat the crowd." The children took off down the hall.

After an early dinner, they went to see a Pixar movie and afterward to an ice cream parlor. As expected, Mary Rose tugged her suitcase into the Duggan's house. Sam Duggan pulled in just as the Taylors were leaving for the hotel. They told him they had arranged to tour a horse farm in Lexington the next day and invited them to come along.

Audrey was exhausted when they arrived at the hotel. Cathy gave her a quick sponge bath, popped her Little Mermaid nightgown over her head, and put on her night diaper. David carried her to the other double bed and kissed her. She was asleep before she finished her prayers.

"Now, wife, tell me all about it—you held it together. I was proud of you, but I saw the steam coming out of your ears."

"Did you hear that woman? She acted like Mary Rose was a leper! 'I hope she's not contagious,' and 'we couldn't find a place for her, with her history!' God, thank You for getting her to Hope House."

"You put her in her place, telling her you were a Hope House girl yourself—what a testimony to what God has done!"

"When I saw you on your knee in front of Benny, I remembered you with Stanley at that age."

"Stanley, the one I courted to catch you?"

"He said you liked him first."

"Yep, but you grew on me."

"And he said, 'Yeah. I saw you kiss her in the orchard.' Not very discreet, Dr. Taylor."

"He also said it's good when married people kiss each other—it makes him feel warm inside. God bless my dad!"

"And your mother."

David glanced over at Audrey. "Let's go take a shower and kiss some more. I really like kissing you."

They were in the shower a long time, doing a lot more than kissing, and he liked that, too.

What to do with Mary Rose?

David became as attached to Mary Rose as Cathy was, and the teenager loved Cathy, who had shared her past with her, explaining she prostituted herself for a college degree and to hide from her parents; whereas, Mary Rose had been trying to take care of her family, and she honored that. Mary Rose attended church with the Hope House girls and her siblings attended church with the Duggans. This afternoon she was at their house.

"One afternoon when we were talking on the phone, Tessa asked me if I'd decided to follow Jesus, Mr. David. Tessa told me she did, and she 'felt warm inside'—and not alone anymore! Cathy gave me a Bible and talks to me about it."

"Maybe this Sunday you should go forward for prayer." And she did. The downside was she felt a growing love for her baby, but she was mature enough to recognize she was too young to provide for one. She also heard the assurances of the Holy Spirit when she chose a family for her baby—he was a boy, and a young coach and his wife were seeking to adopt. She met them, fell in love with them, and wanted them to be with her for the birth.

Meantime, however, David struggled with what they would do with her sisters and Benny. He knew as well as she did the state would never allow her to be guardian—she'd only be fifteen after the baby was born. She'd be placed in foster care herself, and knowing Ms. Fisher, it wouldn't be in the same house.

Mary Rose was only a year younger than Cathy when she faced her decision about Stanley, and she gave David a new and greater appreciation for his wife's courage. Thank God Hope House had enabled Cathy and her mother to reconcile! One night after the kids were down, he looked over his book.

"What are you thinking about Mary Rose? Isn't the baby due next month?"

"He is. She loves the adoptive parents and wants them in the room when she delivers, but God knows what we'll do after her six weeks at Hope House are completed. I hate to turn her over to Kentucky social services—I know Ms. Fisher will never let her be with the kids."

"What can the Foundation do, Cath?"

"What do you mean?"

"Could we build a foster care facility? I'd hire the Duggans to oversee more children. Their little house is full, but we could provide the space and hire some help."

Cathy brightened. "What a fabulous idea! I'll call Kentucky social services on the state level and see if we can work on that."

"It'll take a while to get a building up, but in the meantime, we can rent. We can keep that family together—we have to, for Mary Rose and those children."

Cathy moved over to her husband's chair. He set the book down and raised his arms. "You are a brilliant man!" She leaned her head back and kissed his nose. "And I love you." She met his lips and enjoyed his thorough kiss.

"Let's move this discussion upstairs," he suggested, reaching up to turn off the lamp.

"We can discuss it more in the morning—we might have even better things to do this evening."

"You think?" And they did.

With David's help, after a trip to Frankfort, they filed the paperwork to incorporate a foster care facility. The state was enthusiastic and accommodating, referring them to a professor at Berea College who taught social work. He, in turn, agreed to serve on the Board of the new home and suggested several pastors and community leaders to join the endeavor. They decided to locate the ministry in Berea, thinking students would be good dorm advisors, and they could receive housing and their board as part of their salary.

Going down the steps of the capitol building after their second trip, when all the paperwork was completed, Cathy said she'd miss coming here. "It's a beautiful place, David. I realize how young our country is looking at a mural of Daniel Boone in 1769 exploring the Bluegrass Region."

"I've never seen brass elevators before—complete with the state seal on every one of them! I realized Abraham Lincoln was a native son when I saw the impressive statue in the rotunda." David put his arm around his wife. "I had some good history lessons visiting this place."

"Dr. Morgan said he had several houses for us to look at in Berea. Do we have time?"

"Call your Mom and see if they can keep the kids overnight. I'd enjoy a night alone with my beautiful wife."

She grinned up at him. "That's a good idea!" She called Dr. Morgan, who promised to arrange with a real estate agent to look at several properties the next day. He made hotel reservations for them at the historic Boone Tavern on the college campus, and they met with several board members for dinner that night. Cathy, who was frugal with the Foundation expenses, gratefully accepted a special rate from the manager, who was one of the board members.

As the reality of this children's ministry took shape, the board eagerly participated in discussions and divided up chores. The Dean of students would begin advertising for student employees; the volunteer services coordinator agreed to set up tutors for the children; and the local employment counselor said she'd look for a cook and a janitor. David and Cathy felt the Duggans could oversee the children's care with two college students for dorm counselors. As their dinner meeting closed, Dr. Morgan led them in prayer.

The next morning David and Cathy, with a pastor who was on the board, looked at a few properties, selecting a large older home to lease; he made an offer on a piece of property to build. They conferred at lunch with several of the others, signing the documents before the couple left for home.

"Wow! I never thought we'd get this much done." Cathy bounced on the seat. "Now if only the state will approve our temporary home so we can open."

"We can only house eight or so, but it's a good start," David replied. "You were smart to include that proviso for state approval in the lease. They may have to bend some rules until we can get an approved facility constructed."

"Mr. Jefferson was wonderful about lining up some contractors and getting a bid package together."

"God has given us a good board. Stan would be proud of our first project, don't you think?" David glanced over at her.

"I do—and it rescues our first child prostitute."

"Paying it forward, Cath?"

"Yeah. Some of such were some of us, right?"

He reached across the seat to take her hand, bringing it to his lips. "Have I ever told you how wonderful you are?"

"Mm—maybe, but I like to hear it."

"You are wonderful—a wonderful mother, a fabulous wife, a good social worker, and an amazing person."

"That's laying it on a little thick," she teased.

"I call 'em like I see them."

"You're the best thing that ever happened to me."

"Me? What about John, Beth, Miss Ginny, Missy O'Malley, your mom, Clyde, and Stan Foster?"

"And your mom and dad—all God-given, but you are the best of the best."

"I'd say we have a mutual admiration society going. Let's pray we can get this temporary location going in time for Mary Rose to have a home."

Things did fall together. The rented home didn't have enough bathrooms, so they had to limit their first group to six, but it was approved as a temporary home, to include Mary Rose and her siblings, plus two others. Mary Rose was thrilled the day David and Cathy brought her to the rented house, eager to be with her siblings again. When Cathy hugged her goodbye, it hit her—this meant no more Saturdays at the Taylors, and she sobbed.

"Hey, girl, this is your dream come true," David comforted. "We'll come see you—we have board meetings here every quarter, and if business doesn't bring us down, we'll come visit."

Cathy put her finger under Mary Rose's chin. "You have more hills to climb, sweetie, to get custody of your brother and sisters when you're eighteen. Do well in school—and I'll help you as much as I can."

"I love you, Cathy."

Cathy hugged her tightly and stepped back. "I couldn't be prouder of you."

David was glad he came along, because Cathy couldn't have seen through her tears to drive.

The county allowed the children to attend the school where the new facility would be located, and the state allowed for Mr. Duggan's salary and pension to transfer from the school where he worked in Nicholasville to the new home, so he became the maintenance man. They also granted foster support for the residents. The Foundation approved a salary for Mrs. Duggan, and when they moved into the new building and could house sixteen residents, they hired male and female Berean college students, one of each, as dorm managers.

Cathy's Prayer

Foundation members from the Foster Foundation in Columbus made the trip to Berea to dedicate Grace House in Berea on a glorious Sunday afternoon, almost eight months after the temporary home had established a beginning. Eight more kids were being processed to come to the new building. The one-story structure, with a boys' dorm on one end and a girls' dorm on the other, provided shared living and dining areas in the middle, where the Duggan's apartment was located. Several Hope House girls came in the van and told Cathy later if they'd had a foster mother like Mrs. Duggan, they never would have ended up pregnant.

David draped his arm across the seat, content to let someone with a CDL license drive the rented van. The Foster Foundation members discussed the project and prayed about their next one—maybe a similar home in Ohio? Maybe an after-school tutoring and recreation center? He listened to the buzzing around them and pulled his wife close. "Happy, Mrs. Taylor?"

"Almost perfect."

"Almost?" David looked at his wife closely and noted she held back tears glistening in her eyes. "What?"

"Later."

He waited until they had dropped off the girls at Hope House and had gotten home. Clyde and Audrey's car was in their driveway. "Guess they figured they'd put the kids to bed at home. Reckon they're still awake?"

"Lights are out in the downstairs bedroom—I guess not."

"Tired, honey?" he asked.

"Yeah."

They walked upstairs, checking into each bedroom to look at their sleeping children. Stanley flung his coltish limbs across the bed, and Audrey was curled up in a little ball. "Precious kids, I'm so grateful," he whispered.

Cathy broke away abruptly and almost ran to their bedroom.

David followed her and turned her weeping face to him. "What is it?"

"Audrey is four, David. I thought we'd have another one by now."

"Beth is coming back to Hope House, and you'll have more time—perhaps we should start working on that."

"Why? We haven't tried not to—why haven't we had another?"

"You aren't receiving any condemnation, are you?"

"Maybe . . .." Her eyes were cast down.

David sat on the edge of the bed and drew her down beside him. "Tell you what, if we haven't conceived in three months, we'll go get a check-up. All right? Your last checkup was fine, right?"

"Dr. Reynolds said there was no reason for it, but I feel so barren."

"You aren't barren—look at all the life you've given."

"I want to give you a son."

"And Stanley doesn't qualify?"

She smiled brokenly. "You are so dear. I know he's a son to you."

"I loved him first, remember?"

Her eyes lit up, and she leaned against him. "I remember, but I kinda grew on you."

"You can say that again!" He began to unbutton her blouse. "How about I work on getting you pregnant? That'd be fun." His fingers tangled in her hair as he pulled her down on the bed.

Two months later they were in the doctor's office, telling him they weren't having any success. When he found out how diligently they were trying, he told them to ease up. He suggested they were depleting his sperm count with their efforts and they should wait a week or so before her ovulation.

"Really? I can get her pregnant without trying?"

"No—I'm not talking magic or a virgin birth here." He chuckled. "Go buy some OTC ovulation kits and hold your horses for ten days or so. When the indicator tells you to go for it—well, I don't have to tell you what to do. Take her away for the night and have at it."

The ten days or so were not fun after developing a habit of trying hard, but the "having at it," was wonderful after their enforced abstinence, and two months later Dr. Reynolds confirmed their success.

David drew her toward him when they went to bed. He placed his hand of her still-flat belly, thanking God for this new baby. "Now, I know you want a boy, but I don't want to hear anything out of you if we have a girl. I love Audrey Anne, and God will give us the best child for our family."

"I won't. I just want a healthy baby."

"Scared?"

"A little," she admitted. So, he prayed again.

Little Audrey was delighted to learn they would have a baby in the house, although Cathy had insisted they not tell the kids until after the first trimester because of the miscarriage. Stanley allowed as how he'd been concerned she was getting fat, but Audrey hopped up and down and clapped. Grandmother Audrey and Grandpa Clyde beamed. "Let us know which room to put the second bed," Clyde said. "If it's a boy, we can do bunks, okay Stanley?"

"Beth's Ginger would love to have a little girl to play with when Audrey starts school."

Beth's beautiful daughter had become the next child for the older couple to love. Beth dropped her daughter off on her way to Hope House when she worked part-time, and she or Tom picked her up in the afternoon.

"But girl or boy, it's no matter to us," Clyde assured Cathy.

And that was a good thing, because Benjamin John was born the following summer. David teased the OB, asking how many babies were named after him.

"Not many, really," he replied, "but I know his middle name was after our mutual friend at Hope House." He patted Cathy's hand and stood. "The pediatrician will be in to look at this little fella soon, but he looks great, Cathy. Good job." He shook David's hand. "Looks like your dark hair, Dad."

"I guess they can't all be beautiful like their mom," David said.

"He is beautiful!"

David laughed. "He is. But you'll have to stop saying that soon."

B.J. was a good baby, but a lazy nurser. Unlike Audrey, he wouldn't relieve his mother if she was the least bit engorged. He'd cry and turn his head away instead of pulling on her, and she'd have to express enough milk to enable him to get a good hold. One day, David found her in tears, and gave his son a good talking to, knowing she would come to his defense. While he walked his son, and talked to him, she worked on her breast. Once B.J. started nursing the first, the other one leaked all over her, but it became soft enough for him to grab as well.

"I thought I had this nursing thing down after two."

"Mom says they're all different. Speaking of Mom and Dad, they're flying in this week."

"How can he get away from the orchard?"

"Harvesting begins in two weeks. They're grabbing this time to come meet B.J."

Dalton and Anne arrived Saturday, and Anne pronounced him the spitting image of his father, including his nursing pattern. She took him in her arms after his feeding and burped him.

Audrey Anne took her grandfather's hand and walked him everywhere. Dalton was delighted with his beautiful granddaughter and allowed her to show him everything. He went through the mini-orchard, allowed as how they had a good stand of trees, and gave his son advice on caring for them.

They were included in the reception for Candy and Joe's anniversary and met all the Rodriguez clan. Between her mother and Anne, Cathy could enjoy her first post-baby outing. Stanley had told them all about his friend, Eddie, when they had been back for visits, and now Laura and Ben's Henry had joined the gang, so they felt like they knew the other Hope House babies.

When Dalton noticed how close Candy, Cathy, and Laura were, David told his dad he wished he could meet Missy O'Malley, Cathy's roommate. "When the five of them get together, it's something else! Last time Missy came, Michelle came down from Cleveland Clinic where she's in residency and Laura came over from her home—she's married to our pastor. They each have an amazing story to tell, and God gets all the glory." He told his dad about the fundraiser and how beautifully Missy sang. "There wasn't a dry eye in the place after the girls finished."

"I want to see Hope House, and if we can drive down to Kentucky one day, I'd like to see Grace House. That was a neat thing you did."

"I'm so proud of Cathy, Dad. It can't be easy, giving her testimony, but she sets others free."

"That's what it's all about, son. She's a good girl, your Cathy."

"I know. After her miscarriage, the Hope House counselor asked me if she'd been able to be a good wife. She has. She's a good mom and a good counselor as well."

"Our trials shape us. If we allow God room to move, He makes us ambassadors of His Kingdom." Dalton looked around at the happy, laughing Hispanic family Candy had inherited by marriage. "These folks know how to have fun, don't they?"

"They are good people. Hard-working. Loyal. Generous. Couldn't ask for better friends—but I'd better get little mama home. She looks tired."

David took his family home, but Audrey and Clyde stayed to visit with Martha and Mario. Audrey had taken to calling him Mario because that's what Martha called him. The two women visited often, sharing grandsons, taking them to soccer practice and games, swapping recipes and shopping together. Martha presented B.J. with a christening gown for his dedication.

Cathy didn't feel up to a road trip; her stubborn new son was keeping her awake throughout the night, although Anne helped her with him. David drove Dalton to visit the new foster care facility. David introduced his father to Mary Rose, who happily chatted about school, cooed over the baby pictures and ran back to the room to get recent photos the adoptive parents had sent her of her baby. He was a fine sturdy lad, full of smiles and starting to pull up.

"He's doing good, isn't he, David? I did the right thing, didn't I?"

"He's a fine baby, and he looks healthy and happy. Your gift made his parents very happy, and your brother and sisters are doing well here at Grace House. I'd say you made some excellent choices."

"I couldn't have done it without Cathy. I love her so much! I didn't even want him at first, but when he started to move around..." She sniffed. "I couldn't take care of another one."

"Mary Rose, you're fifteen now." David tucked his hand under her chin and brought it up to look at him. "You have permission to be a teenager. The

Duggans will help you with the little ones. Let them be the mom and dad, and you can be the best big sister in the world."

With a tremulous smile, she said, "Thanks, David. I hope I find someone like you who can love me even though, you know, what I did. I'd like to have a family one day, when I'm ready."

"Cathy has fought some of those same feelings of unworthiness, Mary Rose, but I promise you I never think of those times, buried in the sea of God's forgetfulness. It's Satan, the accuser of the brethren, who holds them over your head. Let them go. One day you will meet the right man for you, and he will love you for who you are."

"You think?"

Dalton took the young teen's hand. "I know. David had to bring Cathy to our place in Washington State so we could convince her to give him a chance when she thought no one could love her."

"You're kidding! She's awesome. I wish I could be half as great as she is."

Dalton took her by the hand as they sat side-by-side on the couch in the living area. "I understand you have the same Heavenly Father. You bear a remarkable resemblance to your Sister in Christ, but when those fiery darts come your way, you be sure to call her to pray with you. Let me tell you about my beautiful wife." And Dalton told Mary Rose the tragedy they overcame in their life.

"Satan thinks he can destroy us, but when the enemy comes in, like a flood the Lord raises His standard against him. God has chosen you, little gal, and don't you forget it. You are a brand plucked from the fire, one of God's trophies."

"Gosh, I hope so." At David's smilingly stern look, she amended, "I know so."

"Did you know Dr. Morgan is securing a special scholarship at Berea College for a Hope House resident? I'll tell Cathy about this grade card. She'll be proud! Maybe you'll be our first winner," David told her.

"I want to make her proud of me."

"She is so proud of you, her buttons pop whenever we talk about you. Miss Martha has to keep sewing them back on!" David put his arm around the girl and pulled her next to his shoulder, dropping a kiss on her forehead. "Now I need to get home."

"I hope she can come and bring that baby soon, and Audrey and Stanley. Thanks for coming."

"We love you, girl."

Mary Rose flung her arms around him. "I know you do. You both believed in me."

Dalton Stanley Taylor

They had barely crossed the Kentucky line when David's cell phone chirped. Dalton picked it up. "Text from Cathy. She wants to know where we are."

"Tell her crossing the state line and almost to I 71. Is everything okay?"

When she responded, Dalton said, "She says she misses you."

"Unusual. I know she loves me, but she's pretty independent."

"Maybe it's a postpartum thing." Dalton's phone dinged and he glanced down. "Uh-oh, something's up. Mama said she's averting a meltdown and not to make unnecessary stops."

David's brow creased. Thank God for cruise control—he wanted to push it up to 80 miles per hour. Dalton prayed and David joined him.

Leaving the suitcases in the car, David jogged to the front door. Anne opened it and pointed to the family room, where he found Cathy with her brave face on, struggling to hold it together. When he dropped on the couch beside her and took her in his arms, the waterfall burst.

Standing in the doorway, Anne took her husband's hand and led him to the downstairs master bedroom, where they were staying, to explain what was happening; and they prayed.

When Cathy's sobs quieted to a shudder, she explained, "Allen called. He said Charlie will be released from prison soon, and if he finds out about Stanley, he might come after him. He's a horrible man, David. He almost killed me. Why are they letting him out of prison? Allen says he's had good behavior and the prisons are overcrowded. I'm scared, David."

"Did he have any suggestions about keeping Stanley safe?"

"He said if you adopted him, he'd go to the judge, explain the situation, and get the records sealed."

David took her hands. "You know I've always wanted to adopt Stanley, but you wanted to keep Stan's name. Do we need to pray about this? Have you talked to our boy?"

"I talked to Allen. He said I gave Stan the gift of a son when he most needed it, and he was sure he'd approve, to protect Stanley."

"And you?"

"You've been Stanley's father. Maybe this is the way it should've been."

Cathy knew David had wanted to adopt her son from the beginning, but when she saw the smile burst across his face, she had no doubts.

"So, all that's left is to talk to Stanley. Where is he?"

"He's at Mom's. I kind of fell apart. I got so scared. Charlie wants the inheritance badly! He was willing to kill once for it."

David drew her into his arms again, kissing her brow. "He knows your name, too, from the trial—we need to get a restraining order, for whatever good they do."

"I'm not as brave as Candy."

David knew Candy had shot Joe's father when he came to kill Martha. "One bridge at a time. First, let's talk to Stanley."

They drove down to Audrey and Clyde's house. Audrey Anne was napping, and they sat the boy down. Glancing from one serious face to another, he asked what was up.

Cathy took his hand. "How would you feel about David adopting you?"

"Wow, that'd be cool. I'd like to have the same name as Audrey and B.J. I'd be a good big brother."

Cathy hugged him. "You already are that."

"The best in the world," David added.

Stanley was anything but dumb. "But why now? Something's come up." He saw tears hovering in his mother's eyes and something else—was it fear?

"Stanley, the dad I've always chosen for you is your grandfather. He adopted you shortly after you were born. He's the wealthy businessman who built those homes in Chicago. His natural son, your birth father, is nothing like him." She shrugged. "For whatever reason. But he's been in prison since you were born. Mr. Overstreet called today and said he's received notification of his release. Stan's son wants the money—his dad's inheritance—which has gone to me and you—and Allen suggested we change your name to protect you."

Stanley took a moment to absorb his new information. "Why did he go to prison?"

"He tried to kill your mother," David said, "and brutalized his father."

Stanley's eyes rounded. "No kidding?" He turned to his mother.

"I was in the hospital for weeks and had surgery. Fortunately, you were a wee seed and unharmed. The trial took place when you were a baby, and we never told him about you."

"Gosh, Mom..."

"So, if it's okay with you, son, we need to move quickly," David said.

"Can he find us? Will he come after Mom?"

David took a deep breath. "It'd take some digging. She's got a new name, since she married me, but if he kept on looking, checking records, he might find her—and you." Stanley paled, and David pulled him into his arms. "We'll do everything in our power to keep you both safe."

"Let's talk to Eddie's Grandpop. He knows about that kind of stuff."

"Great idea, buddy. You're okay with this? I can adopt you?"

Stanley threw his arms around David. "I love you, Dad."

David held him against his chest, looking over his head and winking at Cathy. "Let's do it then!"

They placed a call to Allen and he called the judge in Illinois and a judge in Columbus after he'd talked to their attorney; the wheels were set in motion. Because of Cathy's testimony in the trial, the courts agreed, and a witness protection was set up. They moved in strictest confidence, and the adoption was expedited quickly. For the second time in his young life, Stanley's name was changed. Dalton Stanley Taylor, who would continue to be called Stanley, walked hand in hand down the courthouse steps with the man he'd called dad for six years. Looking up at the tall man, the boy said, "I think Grandpa Dalton liked the name, Dad. I'm proud to be a Taylor—like Uncle Michael, it doesn't matter who gave you birth, it matters who loves you and choses you to be family, right?"

"Absolutely!" David replied, putting his arm around the boy's shoulders. "I've always felt like you were my son, and now I have the name to prove it."

Rod Rodriguez warned them not to become complacent, and they went through repeated drills with the family. After months of quiet, Stanley knew the drill when he was walking Audrey Anne home from the bus and he spotted a strange car in the driveway with Illinois license plates. Having been carefully trained by Eddie's grandfather, he shushed Audrey Anne and led her by the hand to the tool shed in the orchard. He punched speed dial one, and Rod answered. He cautioned the boy to be quiet so he wouldn't tip anyone off. Soon his squad car raced up the highway, stopping at the driveway. Several others followed, and policemen piled out, but it was Rod who circled the house to peer through the back windows.

Taking a breath, he motioned to his men to surround the house. He could see Cathy through the open window. *She is being so brave, God. Keep her strong.*

He saw Cathy curl her fingers into the arm of the couch. It was about time for the children; she must wonder where they were. He heard B.J. wake from his nap and cry.

"Shut him up," Charlie said.

"I have to go upstairs and get him."

"Why aren't the..." he swore, "...children home. I've watched the school, and they should be home by now." He swore again. "Keep that baby quiet."

She rose. "I'll have to get him."

Charlie looked around wildly.

Rod could tell he was on something.

"I'll bring him down, but I have to change him."

"I've cut the phone lines. Don't try anything. If you try to escape, I'll kill the kids when they get here."

"I'll be right back."

As soon as Rod saw Cathy leave the room, he notified his back-up, crashed through the door, his weapon raised, and ordered Charlie to drop the gun.

Charlie fired, again and again, but he was downed in a hail of gunfire as the policemen crashed through the door to protect their beloved captain, on the floor in a pool of blood. One of them dropped to his knees, pulling his belt out to create a makeshift tourniquet.

* * *

Before Cathy could enter the room, another crossed to the foot of the stairs. "Don't go in there, ma'am. It's not a pretty sight."

"Is Officer Rodriguez okay?" she asked.

"He's hit, but he's talking. We've called the ambulance. We need to locate your kids. Your boy called and got us here. Where's the tool shed?"

Holding the baby against her, Cathy ran to the tool shed, one of the men behind her. She threw open the door and found Stanley shielding a crying Audrey Anne.

"We're fine, Mom, but we heard gunshots, and Audrey Anne is scared. Maybe you should hug her or something."

David was running across the orchard toward them. A quick glance showed him they were fine physically, but he saw Stanley with the same brave face his mother had. "You did a good job. Grandpa Rod is very proud."

"Thanks, Dad," the boy said, with a weak grin. "So, everything is good? Mom's here, and we're all okay. Can we get our snack now?"

Cathy giggled, an edge of hysteria in her voice.

The young policeman at the scene of the family reunion tousled the boy's hair. "Let's not go inside the house just now. Do you have some-where to take them?"

"You guys, go get in my car. Let me check on Rod." David dropped a kiss on his wife's brow, where her golden hair met her face. "Are you okay for a minute, honey?"

She clung to him briefly but released him, urging him to check on Rod.

"Is it safe to go in the house?" she asked.

"Yes, ma'am, your assailant is dead. He won't bother you again. Keep the kids out."

An ambulance was in the driveway. As they watched, Rod was carried out on a stretcher, protesting. He wanted to walk on his own, but he wasn't allowed.

David put his family in the car and went to thank his friend.

Rod waved him away. "It's all in a day's work, son. But I'll have to deal with Marta."

"Your wife is meeting you at the hospital, sir," one of the EMT's told him. They lifted him into the ambulance and shut the door, turning on the sirens and speeding away.

"Is he all right?" David asked one of the other men.

"He's a tough old bird, but he lost a lot of blood. We have a tourniquet on him, and he wants to walk!"

To avoid the arriving media, David pulled around back and took the back road to his in-laws. Audrey fixed the after-school snack. Their small house couldn't hold the family, however; they left and went to find a hotel. Candy's house wasn't big enough for them. Merida had a huge hacienda but she and Francisco had been busy filling it with babies. David thanked them all but wanted to keep his family to themselves, together.

Men from the station poured in to donate blood, but Rod only needed one unit. His excellent health and determination to protect Martha from worries fended off shock. He was home the next day, under strict orders for bed rest.

David wisely gave his family time to debrief. He got a suite, but before he got Cathy alone, he spent time with Stanley, listening to his blow by blow account. He praised his quick thinking and the way he protected his sister. The youngster had followed Rod's drills perfectly.

"Is Mom okay, Dad? She was in there with him. Maybe you should be with her."

"Mom told me you wanted her to hold Audrey Anne. Now you deserve a little time."

"I'm fine. Can I read a little before I turn out the light?"

"Do you have anything with you?"

"I got a library book in my book bag. I'm okay, honest."

David walked him to the other bedroom, where Cathy was putting a sleeping Audrey Anne into bed. B.J. was in a crib, oblivious to all the excitement.

She stood, blinking rapidly. She sank onto the bed in front of Stanley. "Thank you for taking care of your sister and for calling Grandpa Rod. You saved your family."

"Grandpa Rod saved us, Mom." He softly touched a purple bruise under her right eye. "He hurt you, didn't he?"

"I'll recover—we're all alive and together, right?"

"He's dead." Stanley said. "He'll never hurt you again."

She pulled him onto her arms and kissed the top of his head.

David switched on the light beside the bed. Quietly he prayed a prayer of thanksgiving for their deliverance, Rod's healing, and protection from bad dreams.

"Mom's not gonna cry in front of me, Dad. She needs to cry. Go on." He waved them off.

Smiling, David offered a high five. Stanley responded with an up top.

Once in their adjoining bedroom, he prepared a chamomile tea and brought it to her. She took the cup and sipped. "I was in the house with that man for forty-five minutes. It seemed like eternity. He was on something. His eyes were wild, and his pupils were pin points. I studied him, and I couldn't see one thing of Stan in him. His nose was big, his eyes were dark brown and deep set, and his eyebrows bushy. His skin was dark. I wonder if he was even Stan's son. She shuddered and set the cup on the table, holding out her arms. He gathered her into his lap, letting her weep, in silence, caressing her back, pushing her beautiful hair back out of the stream of tears and kissing her gently over and over.

"I thought you said he had Stan's eyes and chin? He must be Stan's son. I guess he took after his mother."

"You're right. I'm headed for the shower."

David went into the other bedroom. He slipped the book, Gentle Ben, out of Stanley's hands and snapped off the light. Dropping a kiss on his brow, he thanked God for his brave and beautiful boy.

Cathy was still standing in the shower. He tapped lightly on the bathroom door, so she wouldn't be afraid, and eased into the massage stream with her.

Later, they figured Michael Allen was conceived that night.

About the Author

Charlotte met her husband at Duke University. Married in 1962, they reared six children (four natural, one adopted, and one foster daughter). Their nine grandchildren range in age from adults to a toddler, and four are adopted. A pro-life leader for many years, Charlotte believes God creates every child.

A Phi Beta Kappa graduate of Duke, Charlotte received a Masters of Social Work from the University of North Carolina in 1966. She founded a pregnancy help ministry in 1985, and she's been a Mothers of Preschoolers (MOPS) mentor for twenty years. Her experiences as a wife, social worker, mother, pro-life leader, and MOPS mentor contribute to her inspirational fiction.

She lives with her husband, a practicing orthopedic surgeon, in rural West Virginia. She has published articles and short stories, some of them may be viewed at her website/blog: www.charlottesreaders.com. She has three novels published by Oak Tara, and many articles and short stories published in various magazines. (Her short stories are free and her books may be purchased at Amazon or at her blog.) She is on Facebook and Twitter @Charlotte Snead.